Reframing
Love

By Lyn Ellerbe

Chef Charming

The Intercepted Heart

There Will Be Dancing

Love Beyond Repair

Love's Faithful Embrace

Once Upon a Takeover

Strawberry Kisses

Reframing Love

Lyn Ellerbe

Acknowledgements

Without the encouragement of my family, friends, and readers this continuing adventure of writing would not be continuing! Thank you so much.

Special thanks to my daughter Stephanie and my very good friend Wendy who read and edited *Reframing Love*. That they enjoy my stories is a blessing.

To my husband who reminds me often, "You should be writing…" when day-to-day tasks tend to take up all my time. Thank you for jumping in so I can write!

*Let us hold unswervingly to the
hope we profess,
for he who promised is faithful.*
Hebrews 10:23

A Note to the Reader

This story is a lighthearted, faith-based romance, but it does deal with a situation of family tragedy and rescue from an abusive situation. If any of that may be difficult for you, please feel free to set this book aside and come back to it if and when you're ready.

~*Lyn*

Chapter 1
Thanks for stopping by

Carina Whitley checked her watch for the third time in two minutes. Her lunch appointment couldn't wait, but she needed to let her boss know she was leaving. His meeting was going long, but given his love of conversation, she wasn't surprised. Even though she had only been working for Mr. Garrett Mansfield for a few weeks, she wasn't afraid to interrupt his meeting. He was a kind, older man and treated her well.

"Excuse me Mr. Mansfield," she said, briefly glancing at the man sitting across from the executive's desk who nodded before turning his attention back to his laptop. "I'm going on my lunch break. Do you need anything before I leave?"

"No, no, Miss Whitley," he said. "We're almost done here. I'll let Philip introduce himself to you later. Go ahead and enjoy your lunch."

Carina knew the man in her boss's office was Philip Corelli, the newly hired curator for the Winfield Museum project. The state university system had acquired property near their newest junior college. A wealthy donor, who happened to be Mr. Mansfield's cousin, was an art enthusiast and championed the addition of an art institute and museum. His vision included a high quality, community-centered and family-friendly museum, that welcomed traveling exhibits of well-known masterpieces as well as works from new and local artists. An abandoned warehouse, situated ideally at the edge of campus, set all the plans in motion. The name of the museum was an homage to the Winston College connection and the Mansfield legacy. Carina had been the first hire for the project, and Mr. Corelli was the second.

At her desk, she slipped off her blazer and hung it on the back of her office chair. She changed into comfortable flat shoes and hid her heels in the bottom desk drawer, before heading to the ladies' room downstairs. Reading glasses were tucked into her purse along with the pins that had been holding her carefully groomed hair in place. She shook her long light brown curls loose, enjoying the relief of the casual style. A colorful scarf as a belt and her name tag featuring her nickname 'Ree' completed her transformation.

"I'd make a great spy," Carina stared at her reflection. She was still smiling when she dropped her purse behind the gift store counter. "I'm here, Tess," she called to the store clerk who was assisting a customer.

Twice a week Carina worked in the gift shop during lunch so Tess could meet her fiancé at the campus café. Lincoln Stafford was a grad student in his final semester. Tess worked full time as a teaching assistant in the art department and her duties included staffing the art department's gift store.

Her need to stay busy, a trait that appeared in her early teens, meant Carina had a degree in Business Administration, a certificate in Art Education, years of experience in retail work at an arts and craft store, and recent experience as an executive assistant to the college's president. Convincing Mr. Mansfield she was the best choice for an executive assistant position was easy. Approaching him about implementing more programs for children would be trickier. As soon as she was hired, planning presentations for her ideas filled what little free time she had. Classes for children whose schools no longer had art programs topped her list, along with a permanent room for interactive art activities for kids.

The gift shop was part art gallery and part art supply store. As the museum project grew, the store would expand. Carina was excited to see the growth. The college's winter interim session had just ended, and the spring semester didn't begin for another two weeks, so the business in the shop was slow. Today a mom and her two kids and an older couple were the only shoppers. Tess let the customers know Ree would assist them before she grabbed her lunch and headed out the door. Both sets of shoppers were ready to check out when another customer arrived. Carina immediately recognized him. It was Philip Corelli.

She watched Philip wander the store before he finally joined the short line at the checkout. As the young mom's turn came, Carina greeted the infant giggling happily in his mom's arms.

"You're a cutie," she said.

"Thanks, my mom thinks so, too." A baritone voice replied. Both ladies' heads swerved to see Mr. Corelli's grin. He had bent down to talk with the young boy who had a grip on his mom's skirt.

"This young man seems to be interested in astronomy," Philip said.

The boy's face lit up. "Mommy's buying me stars to glow like the sky in my room." He held up the glow-in-the-dark star set for Philip to inspect. "Aren't they cool?"

"Very cool," Philip said. "Maybe I should get some for my room—or even better, for my new office." Carina choked back a laugh. Mr. Mansfield would *love* that, she thought, picturing the stately, sophisticated man staring at bright green stars on the ceiling of the freshly painted office.

Philip and the young boy continued their conversation as mom checked out. "Bye, Mr. Philip," the youngster called as they left.

"See ya, kiddo." Philip waved before turning to Carina. Seeing her nametag, he smiled. "Ms. Ree, can you please help me? I need a gift for my aunt's birthday. Party's tonight," he said sheepishly.

There were no other customers in the shop, so Carina locked the register and slipped around the counter. "Certainly, Mr. Philip," she said. At his questioning look, she added, "I overheard you introduce yourself to young Tradd." By now she suspected Philip didn't recognize her. She knew he had seen her when he came into the office this morning since he had nodded and smiled. He had also glanced her way when she interrupted the meeting before lunch. If he weren't technically one of her supervisors, teasing him would be fun. Instead she decided to be helpful…but didn't reveal her identity.

"A birthday gift for your aunt?" Carina asked to clarify. Wording her question carefully, she added, "Is she older?"

"Older than me?" he asked. "Yes. I used to call her Auntie Em. It drove her crazy." His evident humor continued as Carina offered her suggestions. Art-inspired

10

knickknacks, stationery sets featuring famous works of art, and a crystal vase were all passed over. They laughed at some of his suggestions which included a set of dolls. His explanation was that the four-year-old princess would love it. *Ah, Auntie 'M' has grandkids,* Carina surmised.

With the attention span of a child, Philip wandered through the shop. An array of adult coloring books he spotted a coffee table book about art through the ages became a strong contender. Philip found a book about ancient Greek statues and held it up. "I've been told I have a classically Greek profile," he said.

It was an observation she made herself weeks ago when his photo came with his resume. The dark curly hair, and light brown eyes were striking, and definitely an indication of his Greek heritage. "Agreed," she said. "Please tell me your firstborn is named Alexander."

"Wow, I haven't heard that one before," Philip replied. "At least not today…and no. I have a cousin named Alexandra, but no firstborn named Alexander." He winked at her. "Yet."

Carina hid her blush by glancing at her watch. No other customers had come in the store, but her stomach was growling and she had hoped to get a chance to sneak in time for her half sandwich and diet soda. "Well, I'm running out of suggestions," she said, as the latest display caught her eye. "Look at this." She held up a boxed set of DVDs. "These documentaries just arrived. They cover art and music through history. Famous actors, and even some comedians, do the narration. I reviewed a couple of the sections, one that covered modern art paired with oldies music, and another featuring classical music and famous masterpieces. They're funny and informative."

"Perfect!" Philip said and picked the art deco,

seventies disco music set. "My aunt will love this one!" He was waiting for Carina to wrap his gift when Tess returned. Carina saw her eyes widen and knew she recognized Philip. A quick shake of her head let Tess know not to say anything.

"Here you go, Mr. Philip," Carina said, handing him his purchase. "Thanks for stopping by. Come again any time." Tess choked back a cough behind Philip's back. Carina shot her a warning glare.

"I will," he said. "Thank you Ms. Ree, Ms. Tess. Have a great afternoon."

At home a few hours later, Carina made a quick change into her dance class clothes. Teaching ballet to five-year-old children was more tiring than her own semi-professional class, but fortunately today was a short session. Afterwards, she'd have enough time to shower and get to her friend's party. Friday nights were her only free nights, but her friendship with Emilia Lazlo was important. The Lazlos taught the Bible study at the church Carina attended. Although they were a few years older than she was, Emilia and her husband Jay, along with their adorable little girl, Sasha, belonged to Carina's small group of friends.

A curly-headed sprite opened the door at the Lazlo's house. "Hello Sassy," Carina said, using the little girl's nickname. "I hear there's a birthday party here tonight."

"Yes! Yes! It's Mommy's birthday! My birthday's not til Easter time." The girl tugged Carina into the kitchen. "Rina's here, Mommy. She brought you a present and flowers! Can I help you open it? When do we get to eat cake? Can I have two hotdogs? Is Uncle Philip coming?"

The rambling continued as she ran back into the living room to join her dad and the other guests.

"Uncle Philip?" Carina asked, a sneaky thought crossing her mind. "Is she talking about the relative you mentioned moving to the area?"

"He's my nephew. His mom is almost fifteen years older than me, so when he was born I was more like an older sister than an aunt. Since we're so close in age it's easier to have Sasha call him Uncle Philip."

The pieces fell in place. Auntie *M* was actually Auntie *Em*, Cousin Alexandra was her daughter Sasha, and the relative was new in town. Carina almost dropped the cup of coffee she'd just poured. "Philip Corelli? Is Philip Corelli your nephew?"

Emilia Lazlo turned slowly. She and her family had been on vacation for two weeks during the time her nephew had moved to the area. He'd teasingly accused them of planning it so they didn't have to help him move into his apartment. They knew he interviewed for a position with a new project in the area, but until he had the job Philip hadn't given them a lot of details. "Yes, Philip Corelli. Don't tell me…"

"Yup, Mr. Corelli is the newest addition to the museum staff."

"That's great," Emilia said. "Have you met him? He's a joy. Hilarious, too. Sassy's favorite person at the moment. Next to you, of course."

Before Carina could answer, the topic of their conversation appeared at the door of the kitchen. "Auntie Em! Happy Birthday!" He kissed Emilia's cheek, then saw that she wasn't alone. "So sorry. Didn't mean to interrupt." Philip's eyes widened as he recognized Carina. "You're Ree, from the gift shop. You know Emmie? I'm her much, much, much younger nephew." He turned to his aunt as he snatched a carrot from the veggie tray Carina was arranging. "Emilia, you didn't tell me you knew someone from the museum."

Emilia's jaw dropped, but the savvy mom understood the situation immediately. Philip didn't recognize Carina as his boss's Executive Assistant. She started to defend herself, "My dear nephew, I most certainly…" when a 'don't say anything look' from Carina stopped her.

"I don't think you did," Philip said as he waved the carrot at Emmie. "I would've remembered, dearest aunt. Nice to see you again, Ree. I apologize for my aunt's lack of information."

"I understand, but if you had I told me Emilia was your Auntie Em," Carina said. "I would've known you have no idea what 'Yes, she's older,' means." She waved the tongs she was using for the vegetables at him. "You told me your aunt was old."

"I said she was older than me," he said, turning toward Carina raising a celery spear to defend against the kitchen utensil.

"You could've clarified," Carina shot back.

Emmie joined in, punching Philip's arm playfully. "You told her I was *old?*"

"Like I said, I told her you were *older than me*, which is true dearest Aunt," he said, his words trailing off as he looked more closely at Carina.

Emmie saw his curiosity increase, so she tasked him with taking the meat to the patio. "Go make yourself useful. Take this out to Jay." She swung around as Philip left the kitchen. "Spill it, sister."

She pulled Carina into the pantry. It was larger than Carina's whole kitchen and afforded them some privacy. After a short explanation, Emilia couldn't stop laughing. Picturing his supposedly 'older' aunt pregnant sent the newly expectant mother into another round of laughter. When she finally caught her breath, she asked, "How on earth did he not know it was you?"

"Watch this," Carina said, twisting her long hair up onto her head. She grabbed Emmie's reading glasses from the kitchen counter which made her blue eyes less noticeable. "Now picture a severe black blazer and high heels."

Emilia was still recovering as Philip returned with the empty meat tray. Carina blushed as he stared at her, his previous confusion turning to recognition. "You! You're not Ree, you're Mr. Mansfield's secretary."

"Executive Assistant," she said, launching into a common explanation she employed. "Although I don't mind the term Secretary—since it derives from the word 'secret'—as in 'keeper of secrets.' I never understood why it became a derogatory term since we have a Secretary of State as our third in line for the Presidency."

"Fourth," he said, falling trap to her distraction technique. "After Vice President and Speaker of the House."

"Which makes them *third* in the line *after* the President."

"Tomayto, tomahto," Philip said. "You must think I'm an idiot."

"Because you were wrong about the Secretary of State?"

At this point, Emmie had to leave to catch her breath. "I'm pregnant. I'm sure this much absurdity isn't good for me."

"Traitor," Philip said. Turning his charm on Carina, he returned to the original topic. "So, you're Ree of The Winston Junior College Art Department Gift Shop *and* Ms. Carina Whitley, stellar *Secretary* to the illustrious Mr. Mansfield, *and* you must also be the famous Rina, my cousin Sasha's favorite person."

"Yes, I am." She smiled. "Nice to officially meet you. I'm sorry I didn't come clean in the gift shop. I couldn't find the right point in our little adventure. I feel silly for thinking your aunt was elderly."

"My apologies," he said as he poured himself a glass of iced tea. "I realized later that I wasn't clear. She's been more like a big sister to me all my life, so I sometimes have to remind myself that she's my aunt." He took the tray of veggies and dip that Carina had finished and followed her to the patio. "Your disguise was perfect. You should be a spy."

"I'll keep that in mind," she said.

Emilia returned to the kitchen in time to hear the end of their conversation. She pulled Carina aside before the evening was over. "You two seem awfully friendly for having just met."

"Shopping for your birthday gift was quite an adventure," Carina said. "He's just a big kid, isn't he?"

"Yes. Yes, he is," Emilia said. *And he may need a time out*, she thought.

Chapter 2
You're in good hands

Sunday morning Philip enjoyed a second cup of coffee as he waited. Emilia had assured him Carina would be at the early church service. His patience was rewarded. He caught her eye, waved her over to the coffee table and handed her a fresh cup.

As she stirred in the creamer and sugar, Carina raised an eyebrow. "Good morning, Mr. Corelli."

"Are you following me, Miss Whitley?"

"Since I've lived here for several years, and attended this church for the last two," she said as she selected a muffin and offered it to him, "I'd say you are the one following me."

"Touché," he said. "Emilia and Sasha are saving me a seat. Would you join us?" Since she normally sat with the family, he hoped she wouldn't refuse.

Emilia protected the pair from unnecessary curiosity by placing herself and Sasha between them. Jay slid in next to Philip after the praise team finished, offering a buffer from the rush of church members that wanted to greet the visitor. Philip didn't mind the attention.

The Lazlos invited Carina to lunch and the pleas of her friend Sassy were too hard to resist. The little girl insisted that Philip and Carina sit on each side of her and entertained them with an imaginative description of what she'd been learning at school. When she wasn't talking, she listened intently.

"Rina, Mommy said Uncle Philip works for you," Sasha said between mouthfuls of French fries.

"Yes, Miss Whitley, please explain how our jobs work," Philip said, grinning over the dark curls.

"Sassy, your Uncle Philip and I both work for Mr. Garrett Mansfield who is in charge of the new museum at the college. It's going to be awesome. There will be art classes and shows and lots of exciting fun for kids, mommies, and daddies."

"And uncles?" Sasha asked. "Can Uncle Philip play, too? He is silly like my dad is."

"I'm sure he is," Carina said. "Although I don't know him very well yet, I think he spends a lot of time being silly."

Sasha's mom and dad laughed at the teasing, but Philip didn't miss the warning look that Emmie sent him. He was in for a lecture later.

Carina excused herself soon after, explaining that she had some research to do before work tomorrow. Philip walked her to her car. "Do I need to talk to Mr. Mansfield about your workload or is this one of your side projects?"

"Side project," she said as she opened her car door. "I'm trying to convince the board to expand the offerings for children to include a permanent activity room. It's a huge drawing point for families. I'm enjoying the process, especially researching the various museums with current installations, so please don't mention my weekend work to him. I'll see you tomorrow."

He watched her drive away, delaying the inevitable grilling he would get back inside the restaurant.

Emilia didn't hesitate. "Philip Andrew Corelli, if you have any thought of toying with the affections of my friend, you will be in for a rude awakening," she said. "She's a joy and gives so much, but she's been through a lot. I don't know the whole story of her upbringing, but she shared with our study group that her parents died when she was young and her father's brother and his wife raised her. It must've been difficult. I think that's part of the reason she stays busy." She watched Philip, seeing his heart melt. He was in danger of forgetting his situation. As she often did with Sasha, she chose frankness. "Does she know about Britney?"

"Relax, Emmie," Philip said. "We met two days ago and have spent all of three hours together. Besides, you know the Britney situation is not normal. Thank you for telling me about Carina's parents. She's a nice, friendly young lady and will be a delightful co-worker. I have no plans for anything else." His aunt and uncle knew he was stretching the truth.

"No plans," Jay said. "Like that always works. Isn't there a quote about 'best laid plans' somewhere?"

"Please be careful, Philip," Emmie said.

"Yes, ma'am, I will."

Carina had stopped for groceries on her way home.

Philip's conversation with his family delayed his own return home. As he rounded the corner of the apartment complex lobby, he almost knocked the groceries from her arms.

"Carina!" Philip steadied her and retrieved the box of crackers that had escaped. "You live here?"

"Yes," she said. She settled one bag on her hip and hit the elevator button. "What are you doing here? Following me again?"

"Of course," he said. "We must be neighbors."

"How delightful," Carina said as the elevator door opened. "Thank you for saving the crackers."

As he watched Carina open her apartment door, down the long hallway from his, Emilia's words haunted him. *Be careful...*

The next morning Philip was surprised, and disappointed, that he didn't catch Carina before she left for work. He wanted to discuss how they'd handle their 'official' introduction this morning. He didn't have her phone number yet so he hoped she was in her office and Mr. Mansfield was running late.

"Hold the elevator, please!" Philip heard the familiar voice just in time. "Thank you, Philip," Carina said as she stepped in, a bit breathless. "I'm running so late. I hope Mr. Mansfield isn't here yet."

"Me, too," Philip said. "Are we going to pretend we haven't met? I'm not sure I'm that good of an actor."

"You should tell him the Ree versus Carina mix-up," she said. "He'll think it's hilarious." She was right.

"So, in the gift shop, on site at the warehouse, and in your church groups, you're 'Ree,' but everywhere else, you're 'Carina'? Is that correct?" Mr. Mansfield asked. Carina confirmed, adding that Philip's young cousin called her Rina.

"That reminds me of a story when there were two J. Petersons on a list of donors," the boss said, launching into one of his many anecdotes. Ten minutes later he wrapped up his story. "I still get embarrassed when I think of how it could have turned out if *Mrs.* James Peterson wasn't as forgiving as the elderly *Judge* Johnson Peterson!"

Hiding a glance at his watch, Philip turned their attention back to their work. If this meeting didn't end soon, he was in danger of missing his appointment with Jasper Ansari, the head contractor. He, Jasper, and Mr. Mansfield toured the museum space, which was in the midst of renovation, several days ago, but Philip's coordination with the contractor was crucial. Either Carina saw Philip's concern, or she was psychic, because she guided the conversation back on topic. She handed him the updated timeline and list of potential donor contacts for Philip. Since the donors, in large part, came from Mr. Mansfield's circle of friends, his attention adjusted quickly. Most on the list had already committed to supporting the project. Carina created it for Philip so that he would be familiar with the main characters at the formal fundraising dinner on Friday evening.

"Carina will be there to help you," Mr. Mansfield said, "accompanied by my nephew Grayson. He's a rapscallion, and my brother has tasked me with reining him in and protecting the family's reputation. Carina volunteered to be his—what did you call it my dear?"

"Confidante and defender," she said. A slight shake of her head halted Philip's obvious question, but his look sent a clear message. He'd be discussing this with her later. Mr. Mansfield's comment assured him that his nephew and Carina's relationship wouldn't be the only topic of conversation.

"Will your fiancée' be attending, Philip?"

Friday's event would be the first large fundraiser for the Winfield Museum. The board hoped that proceeds from the banquet and silent auction would cover the final stages of the renovations. Most of the Mansfield family members were art enthusiasts and collectors. Their large donation of artwork when the patriarch of the family passed away three years ago was the catalyst for the project. The senior Mr. Mansfield, cousin of Garrett and his wife, were life-long supporters of the college and its emphasis on visual and performing arts.

As their meeting wrapped up, Carina excused herself to type out the list of banquet plans that she'd formulated. "I'll get this ready for you to look over this afternoon."

After she left, Mr. Mansfield laid out the remaining hiring issues with Philip until a call from a board member interrupted them. Philip excused himself and settled into the chair beside Carina's desk to wait.

"You first," Philip said.

"I have no idea what you mean," Carina said as she finished updating Mr. Mansfield's daily schedule.

"What's this Grayson guy like and why did you volunteer to date him?"

"That's an awfully personal question for someone you met only days ago. I'm not sure it should be any concern of yours." She continued her work. "Should I ask you about your fiancée?" She asked without looking up.

"Her name is Britney Frost," Philip said. "It's a long story. Although my relationship may not be a concern of yours, I wouldn't mind explaining the situation. I'm surprised Emmie hasn't told you the sordid tale yet." When she didn't respond, he leaned his elbows on the desk. "I could use a friendly ear, Carina."

She met his gaze. "I'm sorry I was so snippy," she said. "I'm not 'dating' Grayson Mansfield. I only agreed to be his date for high profile events. His uncle's oversight is the last chance Grayson will get before his parents do something drastic. They've already cut his trust fund access, which seems to have had some effect, but there are many young women that turn his head, and he doesn't always make good decisions."

"But he hasn't turned yours?" Philip asked.

"Not at all," Carina smiled. "Our relationship guidelines are very clear, and he's behaved himself so far. Besides, I'm not his type." Philip started to ask for clarification, but she turned the interrogation back to him. "Your turn."

He was saved by Mr. Mansfield, who opened his door and waved Philip back into his office. "We'll just be a few minutes, Carina. Then you two can head out to the warehouse."

True to his nature, the few minutes turned into half an hour. Carina had finished all her morning tasks by the time the inner office door opened.

"I have a brunch meeting with a couple of the board members, so you two will have to do the inspecting," Mr. Mansfield said. "It'll be good for Philip to get your input since you've been here since the beginning. Write up your thoughts and suggestions and give them to me this afternoon."

Philip watched as Carina took the abrupt change in her morning plans with no sign of disappointment. Mr. Mansfield was a good boss and cared about his employees—both characteristics that attracted Philip to the position. To see that he was clueless to the inconvenience he caused his assistant was surprising, but didn't seem to bother Carina. Philip would learn later that Mr. Mansfield's actions were never malicious, and Carina verified that he would apologize once he realized he'd overstepped. His kind wife would vouch, also, that he had improved greatly over the years.

"You're in good hands, young man," Mr. Mansfield said as she helped him slip into his overcoat. "Miss Whitley will take excellent care of you."

"I'm sure she will," Philip said, not bothering to hide his grin.

Chapter 3
Your timing is perfect

The rain that had threatened last night finally made its appearance, just as Philip and Carina were halfway to the warehouse. Carina abandoned her high heels and Philip tucked the blueprints under his jacket while they ran for cover. They avoided a soaking but had to suffer teasing from the construction workers who scrambled to locate towels. It was a formal introduction made less embarrassing by Philip's self-deprecating humor. Carina was already a favorite, partly due to the muffins she baked weekly. Now she and Philip were vying for top spot.

The warehouse renovations were nearly complete. After the structural and electrical issues were addressed, the builders moved on quickly to the design phase. Walls were erected, creating separate spaces for the artwork as well as several classrooms. The gift shop would be expanded and connect to the museum via a new hallway.

Seniors in the Interior design program submitted proposals months ago and one of Philip's first tasks was to choose between the finalists. The idea to use current students came from Mrs. Mansfield, since providing opportunities for the students was a priority for the kind-hearted lady. The contest also served to strengthen the connection between the college and the museum as the interior designers were asked to involve as many other students as possible. Visual and digital artists, drafting majors, and architects teamed up. The submissions were exceptional. When Philip had glanced through them over the weekend, he knew why Carina had said that she didn't envy him the job of deciding.

"Well, Mr. Corelli," she said after she slipped her shoes back on, "are you ready for your guided tour? I know you've walked through on your own, but Jasper has offered to show you around."

Jasper Ansari, the head contractor, offered cups of hot chocolate from the break area set up in one of the completed rooms. "Mr. Corelli, we're excited about our progress and are optimistic about meeting the deadlines. Are there any areas you have questions about?"

"This looks magnificent. Please, sir, lead the way," Philip said. "Carina, are you joining us? I'd value your perspective."

"I'll catch up with you," she said. "I want to check on the classroom I hope to claim for the littlest artists. Is that okay?"

"Of course, ma'am," Philip said, saluting her with his cup of cocoa. "I see where I fall on your list of favorites. Right behind preschoolers and kindergartners." Seeing her raised eyebrows, he sighed. "No, don't tell me. I'm much further down this list, right?"

She laughed and waved him towards Jasper. "Behave and your standing may improve."

The lead carpenter, Tyrone Watson, joined Carina as she inspected her favorite room. "Does it meet with your approval, Ree? Any changes you want, I'll do. Your wish is my command, milady." Tyrone was a handsome man and she knew his flirting was harmless. They had gone on a couple of dates before she had agreed to help Mr. Mansfield's nephew. He was one of only a few that knew the true nature of that relationship. He'd jokingly asked her to promise not to fall in love with 'that scamp,' before she gave him a chance first. The two had settled on friendship for now. Carina viewed it as a permanent label, but she thought Tyrone might still be hopeful.

Their echoing laughter caught Philip's attention across the warehouse. When she finally joined him and Jasper, he debated asking about her companion, but decided to wait. *Let it go, Philip. It's none of your business.*

They toured the rest of the building, then laid out the plans on a table Tyrone cleared off for them. It was a working copy, so Philip made notes on the blueprint as they talked.

"So, this is the art education room?" He circled the classroom that Carina and the carpenter had just visited.

"Well," Carina said, "that's *my* hope, but I'm not sure the board and Mr. Mansfield have agreed. He told me that I'd have to consult the new guy before final decisions were made. I hear he's a reasonable man, but you know him best. Will he be open to fulfilling all my dreams and plans?"

Philip watched the blush as she realized the possible double meaning in her words. "What dreams and plans are those, Miss Whitley?"

"Stop it," she said, busying herself with the other pages of design plans. "You know what I mean. My hopes for a vibrant children's art program."

"Ah, of course," he said, smiling at her discomfort. "Those plans. Yes, I'm sure the ogre of a manager will be open to all reasonable suggestions...for the museum."

She ignored his teasing and flipped to the spreadsheet she had created with the checklist of tasks to be completed before the opening later in the spring. Philip had already added a few more, which was to be expected as he assessed the project. One line caught her eye.

"Reframing the artwork?" Carina asked. "Did you want all the artwork reframed in a particular style or were you thinking about the submissions from amateur artists that come in without mats or frames?"

"Still in the contemplation stage, but probably some of both," he said. "Would you like to be included in those discussions?"

"If you like, I can participate as an interested bystander," she said, "unless you need me to help with framing. I'm a certified picture framer."

"Of course you are." Philip put down his pen and folded his arms. "How does an executive assistant for a university have an artwork framing certificate? Those aren't easy to come by."

"I have an eclectic background, sir. My friends say I'm a perpetual student, which isn't quite true, but I do like learning new things. Plus, I like to stay busy," she said. "I need to, in order to stay out of trouble."

"That I can believe," Philip said. He bopped her on the head with one of the rolled blueprints. "Thanks for the warning."

The next morning Tyrone met Carina in one of the classrooms to set up an area for her to frame the community and college artwork submissions. As they pushed tables together, Tyrone posed a question. "Ree, can I ask you for a favor?"

"Certainly," Carina said.

"I know our dates didn't turn out to be the magical evenings we had planned," he said, laughing when he saw Carina bite her lip to hide her own laughter. "I'm glad you decided we could be friends, despite my blunders."

Their two dates weren't disasters, but halfway through the second one, they both knew that friendship was where they'd remain. "I don't apply the label 'friend' lightly, Tyrone, so please don't hesitate to ask for help. What do you need?"

Tyrone's mood during their dates stemmed from a recent break up. He had fallen hard for a girl introduced to him by a cousin. He and Kendra had dated for a few weeks when Tyrone had to leave town to handle a family emergency. His grandmother had fallen ill suddenly, and his parents needed his help.

Because the relationship was so new, he didn't communicate well with her, thinking it was too early to involve her in family concerns. When he returned and reached out, she seemed uninterested in resuming their relationship. "My cousin says she explained the situation to Kendra and suggested I try again. I have a plan."

Kendra played trivia with a group of friends on Friday nights at a local diner. Tyrone suggested he and Carina have dinner there.

"Would it be a problem if she sees me with you?" Carina asked. "Will that make her jealous or make her avoid you?"

"I thought of that," Tyrone said. "If you bring the files and blueprints for the children's rooms, we can make it a working dinner. I think if I can get her to talk to me, we'll be okay."

"Excellent plan, my friend," Carina said. "Plus, I love Cisco's loaded French fries, and I haven't been there in ages."

"Great! It's a date," he said with a wink. "I'll pick you up on Friday at seven."

Neither of them noticed Philip in the shadows of the hallway. Back in his office minutes later, he stared out the window until he decided the risk was greater worthwhile. He called Emmie to cancel his normal Friday dinner appointment.

"What's up dearest nephew?" Emmie asked.

"I'm most likely getting ready to make a huge mistake," he said, stopping her as she started to respond. "Nope, don't say anything. I need to do this."

When he heard her sigh, he tried to calm her fears. "Don't worry, I'll fill you in later, and you can tell me what an idiot I am."

As planned, Carina spread the blueprint out on the restaurant table in front of Tyrone. He placed himself strategically in Kendra's line of sight. When she smiled, he made his way over to her table and invited her to join him and Carina.

"She's joining us," Tyrone said as he rejoined Carina. She squeezed his hand, a gesture timed with the perfection of a soap opera...just as Philip entered the diner.

Philip had spotted Carina through the restaurant's window. When he paused inside the door, Tyrone waved him over. Philip pulled out a chair and started stacking the files and plans to make room on the table. He saw Carina's frown out of the corner of his eye. Any interchange was delayed when Kendra returned to join them.

Tyrone made the introductions.

"Kendra, this is Philip Corelli, head curator of the new museum," Tyrone said. "Philip, this is Kendra."

"So, do you two work together?" Kendra asked.

"Yes," they replied in unison. "Jinx," Carina said. Philip thought he saw a blush, but soon realized it wasn't embarrassment. "Your timing is perfect as usual, Philip. Our order is ready. You can help me collect it after you place yours." Pushing out of her chair, she gave him no ability to refuse. As soon as they were out of earshot, Carina made her displeasure clear.

"What were you thinking? It's obvious you're here to spy on us," she said as she collected the condiments and refilled her drink. "I have no idea how you thought eavesdropping—which it's clear you were doing when Tyrone and I made our plans—was a good idea. To follow that with showing up here is incorrigible."

"Are you done?" Philip asked. Even on their short acquaintance, Philip could tell she wasn't as angry as her words implied, but he was sorry he'd upset her. "Could you look at me? Please?"

When she did, his regret was clear. She shook her head and turned away. "Go order your food. I'll wait." She collected her order and when he reached her side, she let him take her tray. "Those puppy dog eyes won't change my mind, sir."

"I didn't ace my course in linguistics, but I think I remember that 'incorrigible' means you're not happy with me at all." Philip said. "Are you sure I can't make it up to you?"

"Yes," she said before they returned to the table. "Just sit and keep quiet. I'm helping Tyrone. He's smitten and wants my opinion of this young lady. He messed up early in their relationship and hopes she's forgiven him. We're optimistic, so don't do anything to jeopardize it."

"First I'm in trouble for eavesdropping, then stalking, and now I'm possibly responsible for ruining Tyrone's happiness," Philip said. One dark brow rose as he leaned toward her. "Are you sure you want me to stay?" She ignored him.

The rest of the dinner was pleasant, both Carina and Philip offering award winning performances. Kendra and Tyrone entertained them by taking turns answering the trivia questions. Philip and Carina joined in and by the end Tyrone proposed they come one week and compete for real.

"Sounds good," Philip said. He glanced at Carina who was moving fries around her plate. She didn't look up. Shortly after nine, Carina tried to hide a yawn, and Philip noticed.

"I have an early day tomorrow, and it looks like it's past Miss Whitley's bedtime," he said. Leaning closer to her he added, "May I offer you a ride home, Carina?" Tyrone, ever the gentleman, started to object, but Carina stopped him.

"We live in the same apartment building, so it's no problem," she said. She gathered her files and the blueprints, then hugged Kendra. "It was so nice to meet you. Enjoy the rest of your evening. Thank you, Tyrone. I'll talk to you about the plans next week."

The ride home was as combative as Philip feared, but he was prepared. He let Carina rail again about interrupting her fake date, before landing his one salvo. "It's okay for you to protect Grayson, look out for Tyrone and, I suspect, to be curious about my relationship with Britney, but I'm not allowed to care about you?"

"So you're admitting that you eavesdropped and followed us to the restaurant?" Her accusations gained back her advantage.

"I never denied it," he said. "Now you need to admit that my being there aided your objective. How long would it have taken for you to be the third wheel at the table?" When she didn't respond he winked at her over the rim of his drink. "You can thank me later."

As they pulled up to their apartment complex, Philip came around to help her from the car, but she had scrambled out, even with her satchel of files and to-go box. His brow furrowed as he saw a look of fear. Was it fear, or was she still angry? He stepped back and followed her inside. As they exited the elevator, after a silent ride, he held out his hand. "Let me carry something, Carina. Please, so I know you forgive me."

"I forgive you," she said, but didn't relinquish her satchel or box. "I'm sorry I got so angry. I'll see you on Sunday."

Chapter 4
Is he a problem?

Carina texted Mira Goodwin after she got home from the restaurant. Apologizing for the lateness, she asked if she could treat Mira to breakfast. Her long-time confidante responded immediately.

"I was thinking about you today. How cool is that?" Mira said. "Yes, let's do it!"

Mira was an unusual counselor. The older woman had worked with Carina since the event that removed her from her guardian's home. The regular meetings during Carina's childhood lessened to two to three a year in high school, and less often in college. Only when an event triggered fear or doubts did Carina reach out after college. Until recently, those conversations were by phone.

Mira tried to not have favorite patients, but Carina was special. The counselor met a scared, ten-year-old girl who was still confused about losing her parents nearly four years before. That young girl had grown into a confident young lady, who was aware of her weaknesses and worked to overcome them. When Mira's elderly parents needed to move to an assisted living home, she and her husband relocated to Atlanta. Carina's move to the distant suburb of that city a few months before, gave them the chance for in-person visits.

The friends enjoyed hot chocolate and cinnamon rolls, which provided a welcome reprieve from the dreary Saturday morning.

"It's been a while since we talked, young lady," Mira said. "What caused the sudden need to meet today? Anything to do with your boss's nephew?" Carina had called several weeks ago and talked to Mira when Mr. Mansfield asked her to help with Grayson.

Carina winced. "Not really," she said, assuring Mira that Grayson had behaved so far. Today she wanted to talk about how to handle Philip.

"How to 'handle' Philip? Your newly hired head curator? Is he a problem?" Mira led the conversation back to their previous ones. She had questioned Carina's volunteering to shepherd her boss's nephew when she first learned of the plan. Mira knew Carina felt a need to protect people, both vulnerable ones and ones that had tendencies to misbehave. She knew the underlying reason but wanted Carina to see the pattern she was repeating.

"Are you hiding behind that wall again? I thought you'd opened up a hole, at least a small one, and stepped through." Mira paused as the waitress refilled their mugs. "Why does Philip need protection?"

"He doesn't," Carina said. "I just feel bad for him. He seems unhappy whenever his girlfriend is mentioned."

Mira interpreted Carina's hesitation accurately.

"You know why, or suspect you know, but aren't comfortable sharing that, correct?" Carina nodded. "You feel safe with him, don't you?" Another nod. "Does that make you uncomfortable or does it worry you that it doesn't make you uncomfortable."

"You're very good at this, you know." Carina said. "Yes, I like him. He's funny, friendly, and I'm comfortable around him. This is different than my fake relationship with Grayson. That's more like babysitting than anything. I have other friends that are men. Why do I feel so protective of Philip so soon? Is it a problem that he's got a girlfriend? Why is this so confusing?"

Mira laughed. "Slow down. I think this is good. You've made a friend that happens to be male, but you're smart enough to not get involved too deeply," she said. "Why don't you concentrate on being a good friend and praying for him? Don't worry about solving his problems. Someone more powerful cares even more than you do."

Mira realized this was different than any other of Carina's visits. A corner had been turned. Usually she sought relationships where she was in control—by being the caregiver or the crucial part of a bigger plan. The fact that she didn't know Philip had a girlfriend before she allowed herself to be drawn in, was important. Being the needed one was safer than being vulnerable. It was a major shift, but not one that was easily managed. Mira secretly hoped their next conversation would include *It's okay to be more than friends with a man, Carina.*

The next week was hectic for the entire staff. Carina planned to spend most of Wednesday and all of Thursday at the banquet site. Being on hand for vendor deliveries, decorating, and set up were part of the 'other duties as assigned,' qualification in her job description. This wasn't the first museum event, but it was the largest. Carina welcomed the change of routine. People that didn't know Carina well described her as quietly efficient. Although that was an accurate description, it wasn't complete. Carina loved being busy and loved being around people. Because she didn't dominate conversations and tried to stay out of the limelight, they assumed she didn't like these big events. That was far from the truth.

By mid-morning Wednesday the facility looked more like a high society soiree than the empty banquet hall that greeted Carina on Tuesday. The current background music, though, didn't match the decorations. Pop music—a mixture of oldies and current top forty songs—filled the event area as Carina and the crew of volunteers mapped out the tables and dance floor. The group took a break before lunch and Carina cued up some line dances. The laughter from the impromptu party reached the outer doors as Philip stopped by to check on the progress. He stood in the ballroom door and watched the fun.

"C'mon, boss! Join us," one of the crew called. As the song ended, Carina waved him over. Another song was beginning. She grabbed his hand and pulled him into the line. The shadow of the diner fight had evaporated.

"Do you know this one?" She asked. "If not, just follow me." Line dancing had been popular for several years and Philip was familiar with it, but not an aficionado by any means. But he could follow directions. It didn't take him long to catch on. He was a natural. Their lunch delivery arrived after the next dance. They invited Philip to join them.

Philip had been memorizing lists of biographies of the high-end donors—both current and potential. It was his least favorite task and one he hoped to re-gift to Mr. Mansfield soon. The patriarch was a natural at convincing people to financially support causes. He didn't pressure donors, but genuinely cared about the arts and had surrounded himself with generous friends. As much as Philip disliked making phone calls, he was learning a lot. Still, the dance party was a perfect escape.

The camaraderie was encouraging. Philip had hoped for a work environment where the employees loved their job. The picnic style lunch was ideal. Carina spread a tarp on the ballroom floor and arranged the bags of subs, chips, and cookies within everyone's reach. It was one of the most enjoyable meals Philip had experienced.

Carina excused the group to get back to decorating while she cleaned up. Philip insisted on helping. "Don't you need to get back to work?" She asked as she handed him the folded tarp. "Or do you get to do whatever you want since you're the head honcho now?"

"Head honcho. Hmm, I like that one. You should call me that from now on," he said as he gathered the lunch leftovers. "Do you want me to put these in the kitchen here or at the office?"

"Here. A couple of the crew will take them home." she said. "Thanks for joining our party. Did you want a tour of the facility?"

"Yes, if you have time," he said. "The place looks great."

"We're almost done with the decorating. The greenery will come later today, and I'll pick up the flowers Friday morning." Carina began the inspection in the kitchen. Philip offered to read off the inventory sheet as she checked the food supplies that were delivered earlier.

"You're not working Friday afternoon are you?" Philip asked. Mr. Mansfield had given the entire staff Friday afternoon off. "So everyone can do all their primping and preening for the evening."

"No, but I'll be back here early to check on everything," she said. "I'm looking forward to the event. It's so important to the project. I hope it goes well and we raise the funds we need."

Philip was thankful she didn't ask him if he was looking forward to the event. He was torn. Normally these were highlights of his job. This one would be less so. Britney and her parents would be there.

A single phone call changed his mind and solidified his dread.

"I don't know what to do Emmie," Philip said as he paced his office floor. "Mr. and Mrs. Frost aren't coming as they originally planned, but Britney still is. She wants to stay for the weekend, but not with the business associates her parents had arranged." There were no hotel rooms available because of several large events happening in the metro area over the weekend. "What do I do? Of course, Britney insists she can stay with me," he said. "But as always, I've refused. I don't know why she can't get it through her head. That's *not* going to happen. Ever."

"Knock, knock." The voice at the door was welcome. It was Carina. She saw he was on the phone and apologized. "Sorry. I can come back later."

"Emmie, I've gotta go. Carina's here. Yes, I will. I'll call you later if I figure something out." Philip waved her into the office. "Emmie says hello."

Carina handed him the updated checklist for the event and the checks that needed his signature. "Everything okay?" She asked.

After less than a week as colleagues, her concern was touching. "There's a small glitch, but I'll figure it out. You don't happen to have a friend that works in the hotel business and has a spare room for this weekend?" He explained the situation, trying his best to keep his disappointment out of his tone. *How bad is it that I'm dreading spending time with my 'fiancée'?* He made a mental note to ask Emmie and their church Bible study group to pray again for his situation.

"She can stay with me," Carina said.

Philip almost dropped the coffee he was handing to her. "What? You've got to be kidding. No. Absolutely not. I'd never ask you to do that."

"You didn't ask," she said as she wiped up the spilled coffee. "I offered."

They spent the next few minutes arguing. Carina won. Her one-bedroom apartment had a sleeper sofa that was surprisingly comfortable according to her college roommate, who had visited several times. "Will she need to come to my place early to get dressed? I can leave a key for her at the security desk." The arrangements were made, and a dejected Philip watched Carina leave his office.

What have I done?

Chapter 5
Is this a challenge?

The banquet hall had a private dressing area, used most often by bridal parties. Tonight, Carina and Mrs. Mansfield had the area all to themselves. Carina had decided to stay after she finished the last-minute decorating, and her boss's wife had volunteered to help arrange the flowers. The older lady was one of the sweetest people Carina knew. She called herself the "Gram of the office," and treated everyone like family.

Minutes before the guests arrived, Carina helped Mrs. Mansfield by fastening her emerald necklace. The dark green and gold gown was a perfect choice for the boss's wife, and Carina had helped Mr. Mansfield pick out a tie to match his wife's dress.

Carina's dress was one her college roommate had found at a thrift shop. So sure it would look great on Carina, she had called from the store, sent photos, and tried it on herself. They wore the same size, but she was a couple inches shorter than Carina. "It's too long for me, so I think it will be ideal for you. It still has the tags on it!" Her pick was flawless. The dress looked like it had been made specifically for Carina.

The satin mocha brown dress perfectly

complemented her hair. It was slightly off the shoulder, A-line, with a not too deep V-neck. Mrs. Mansfield gasped when Carina came out of the dressing room. "Oh my, young lady! You look like you stepped out of a magazine!"

The splurge on a hairdresser was a gift from Mr. and Mrs. Mansfield for all her extra work. She had tried to refuse the gift, but knew pushing back too much would offend the kind couple. The hairdresser asked her to bring a picture of herself in the dress. After combing out Carina's long hair, the stylist recommended a 'messy bun.' Carina was concerned by the name, but the final result was lovely. With thin loose strands framing each side of her face, the style was perfect for her naturally curly hair. A gold and pearl hairclip that matched her pendant was a final touch.

The stranger staring at her in the mirror was encouraging, not frightening as she expected.

"Let's go have a ball," Mrs. Mansfield said. Taking Carina's offered arm, the pair joined Mr. Mansfield and his nephew in the still-empty banquet hall.

Grayson smiled and bowed over her hand. "You look lovely tonight Miss Whitley. Thank you for allowing me to accompany you." Carina retrieved her hand. He would remember their agreement, but played his role well in front of his uncle. He'd be disappointed to know he wasn't fooling anyone…except perhaps Philip.

As the ladies came through the double doors at the back of the room, Philip dropped the seating chart he was memorizing. And he forgot how to breathe as he saw Carina. He took a step toward the group but stopped when he saw her date's greeting. Any further response was cut short as the ballroom doors opened to let in the waiting guests.

Mr. and Mrs. Mansfield greeted each guest as they entered. A bar was open and an appetizer table was set up in one corner. Carina mingled and made sure everyone was able to find their seats. As the time for dinner service neared, Philip intercepted her.

Grayson stayed by Carina's side, as his uncle had instructed, but with Philip's presence, he saw an escape. "Carina, I'll go get us our drinks and then find our table—is that okay?" Grayson said. "I had an early flight so I'm pretty beat." He'd been eyeing the bar since it opened. His parents hadn't arrived yet, and his window of opportunity for misbehavior was short. Carina glanced from him to Philip and back to the guests wandering around looking at place cards.

"That'd be great. I'll take a club soda, with a lime, please," she said. "I need to keep a clear head tonight, especially since I get to meet your parents tonight." Her comment landed its mark as Grayson nodded guiltily.

Philip pulled out the seating chart that he'd abandoned earlier. "I can help the guests. I've got the chart memorized."

Carina thanked him for his help, but knowing most of the guests were still greeting each other, pointed to the appetizer table.

"I'm starving," she said around a mouthful of a

lobster puff. "I haven't eaten since breakfast. I'm glad the background music is loud enough so no one can hear my stomach growling."

"Oh, that's what that sound was," Philip said as he popped a cherry tomato into his mouth.

Carina started to make a face at him, but stopped in time as one of the biggest donors, Professor Patel, approached them. The Art History professor was a favorite, and wholly supported Carina's dreams for the museum to provide opportunities for children who would otherwise not be exposed to the arts. Carina had pages of research, including a list of all the local schools that had dropped their art programs.

She introduced Professor Patel and his wife to Philip, then led them to their table. Since she oversaw the seating arrangements, the Patels were at her table, along with Emmie and Jay. Philip was across the dance floor. He caught her eye, picked up his place card and pretended to wipe away a tear. She grinned and mouthed, "Sorry." He saluted her but his smile was suddenly replaced by a frown. Carina followed his gaze and saw a stunning woman enter the room. *This must be Britney*, she thought.

Tall, blonde, regal. She greeted Philip with a kiss that would've embarrassed even the boldest of men. His discomfort was evident, but Carina was one of only a few that had seen the embrace.

Philip detangled himself from Britney and led her to Mr. Mansfield's table for introductions. Carina decided to help, so she excused herself and joined the pair.

"Carina, have you met Philip's fiancée? This is Britney Frost." Mrs. Mansfield said, saving Philip from the awkward introduction. "Britney, this is Carina Whitley. She's my husband's Executive Assistant, which we all know means she's the glue that holds the project together."

"Hear, hear," Mr. Mansfield said. "Wouldn't you agree, Philip?"

He was still distracted by hearing the term '*Fiancée*'—he rarely used the word. *Girlfriend* was difficult enough to say.

"Yes," Philip said, not venturing anything further. The evidence was clear that Britney had no idea of the level of Philip and Carina's friendship. As far as she knew, this was simply the woman whose apartment she appropriated. She raked a gaze up and down Carina, taking in her outfit, shoes, hair, and jewelry. Britney's curled lip, which she didn't try to hide, dismissed Carina as no competition. When she met Carina's eyes, though, a beautiful smile appeared. The transformation was instantaneous.

"So nice to meet you Carina," Britney said. "You are so kind to host me this weekend. I hope I won't be too much trouble."

"Oh, no trouble, Miss Frost," Carina said. "Please let me know if you need anything at all." Seeing a pair of donors heading their way, likely wishing to speak to Philip, Carina made an impromptu offer. "I see that Philip is about to be claimed by some gentleman. I'm sure they want to speak to our new Curator about the collection. I'd love to introduce you to some of the other guests." Based on comments she'd heard from Emilia, she added, "Many are from the inner circles of society. I know they'd love to meet you." It was a good move. The young lady was charming and caught the eye of several young gentleman, Grayson included. Carina steered Britney in another direction.

When Carina delivered Britney to Philip's side as the dinner service started, he leaned over, out of Britney's line of sight, and whispered, "Thank you."

The dinner was delicious. Philip watched Carina's group with a twinge of jealousy, but forced himself to be pleasant to all his table mates, even Britney. She wasn't an evil person, but their situation was solely her doing. Being a man raised to value integrity wasn't always an easy path.

During the dessert course Mr. Mansfield gave a short speech and introduced the new Head Curator. Philip offered his thanks for their generosity, reminded the guests about the silent auction items displayed in the next room and even humorously offered recommendations. "If any of you are feeling particularly sorry for a new arrival to your beautiful community, the large landscape painting would look nice over the fireplace of the house I hope to find. I'd be forever grateful." When the laughter died down, he introduced the band and invited everyone to enjoy the music before surprising all but apparently Mr. Mansfield. "I've been told there will be several songs that invite—perhaps demand—group participation. I was taught several line dances this week and I'm looking forward to putting the new knowledge to use.

Enjoy the rest of the evening, and again, thank you!"

Dessert and dancing filled the next hour. The line dancing was a hit, if somewhat disconcerting seeing tuxedo clad men and women in fancy ball gowns doing the electric slide. Of course Carina and Philip participated but Britney's displeasure was evident. Carina frowned at him until he got the message. The next song was a slow ballad. Philip and Britney took the floor, as did Carina and Grayson. They crossed paths and Britney sent the young Mr. Mansfield a smile that he obviously interpreted as an invitation.

"Is that Philip's girlfriend? Are they serious?" Grayson asked, not seeing Carina's frown. How could she discourage his flirtation addiction and give Philip a break at the same time?

"Yes. Her name is Britney Frost," she said. "I'll introduce you. We can look over the auction items since I'm sure Philip needs to check on the bidding progress. Remember that you're my date, not hers, and that she's engaged." The reminder got his attention. He nodded. Carina was hopeful, but not convinced he would behave as well as his parents and uncle expected.

Introductions were made and the four perused the auction items together. Britney's full attention turned to Grayson. As they moved away, Philip thanked Carina again for intervening.

"How is your evening with young Mansfield?" Philip asked as they watched their dates sharing a laugh and enjoying another cocktail. "They make a handsome pair, don't they?" Carina nodded but remained silent.

"Why did you blush when you introduced me to him?" Philip asked. "He's behaving himself, isn't he?"

"Yes, he is. His parents are here so he's being extra careful. If I blushed, which I doubt, it was because I didn't want you to think I was so lacking in rationality to actually be interested in him," she said as she fingered a delicate crystal vase that was among the auction items. Over her shoulder she dismissed his line of interrogation with a final comment. "I explained our agreement earlier and also you should know I'm not that naïve."

Philip saw Britney and Grayson head to the dance floor and turned to Carina. "Shall we? I know you can do the Cupid Shuffle, but can you waltz?"

"Is this a challenge Mr. Corelli? You watched me waltz with Grayson. Are you saying I won't be able to waltz with *you?* Is it me you're worried about or yourself?"

Emilia overhead their banter as they passed her table. "Hey Emmie," Philip said. "Do you need anything before I show off with Miss Whitley on the dance floor?"

"Nope," Emilia said. "Jay is getting me another lime soda. I'm pretending it's a margarita." She patted her baby bump. "Have fun, you two." As Carina turned away, Emmie glared at Philip. He donned his best impression of Sasha's 'it wasn't me' look. She mouthed, *'Behave.'*

The band struck up a popular love song. "How ironic," Philip mumbled.

"What?" Carina asked.

"Nothing important," he said as he pulled her into a

loose embrace, which he loosened even more when he felt her tense. As they made a turn, he moved slightly closer, partly because of the crowded dancefloor and partly because she had relaxed. He needed a distraction. "How do you think the evening is going?"

"Very well, if the current auction bids are any indication," she said. As they crossed paths with their boss and his wife, she waved at Mrs. Mansfield. "Mr. Mansfield seems satisfied. How is everything going on your end?" Carina asked. When he didn't answer right away, she changed topics. "Britney said she got settled in with no problems. She's quite stunning, you know."

"Yes, she is," Philip said.

"She seems nice," Carina said.

"Yes, she does," Philip's cryptic tone communicated more than he intended. "Thank you again for letting her stay with you." They danced in silence until the ending of the song neared.

"When do I get the long story, Philip?" Carina asked.

"Soon," he said.

In a wise move, Philip asked Emmie and Jay to drop Britney at Carina's apartment. Grayson had offered but Philip had seen the way Carina's 'boyfriend' looked at Britney. Better to not offer more temptation.

"But if those two became a couple, wouldn't that solve your problem?" Emmie asked.

"Yes, but not Carina's. She's agreed to help him reform, or at least to start to see the error of his ways,"

Philip said. "I'm leery of the guy, but Carina thinks he's making progress. Honestly, I feel like I need to protect him from Britney, but until I know better, based on his reputation, I wouldn't wish him on anyone. Even Britney."

"And definitely not Carina," Jay muttered, earning him an elbow in the ribs from his wife.

Philip walked Britney to his family's car. "I'll be here late packing the auction items for delivery to the winners, and cleaning up. I'll talk to you in the morning." He closed the car door and turned to find a frowning aunt. She wasn't more than a few years older, but sometimes acted like a mama bear. This was one of those times.

"I'll say it again, Philip," Emmie said. "Be careful. Carina and Grayson are not your business." She held up her hand to stop his response. "I know, I know. We've had the 'guys can see things in guys that girls don't see and vice versa' argument. Still, you shouldn't get too involved in another young lady's dating life—even if it is only out of concern for her. You are technically engaged to someone else, you know."

"Believe me, I remember," Philip said, as he turned and saw Britney watching him. Her elegantly raised eyebrow meant there would be a conversation later.

Chapter 6
It keeps me out of trouble

Britney was asleep when Carina left the next morning, but she had mentioned a breakfast meeting with a sorority sister before spending the rest of the day with Philip. *I hope it's a carefree day for him,* she thought, and felt guilty that she doubted it would be.

Carina's Saturday morning ballet class was the only thing on her schedule, so afterwards she grabbed a quick take-out salad and decided to tackle the last of the banquet clean up.

As she pulled up to the building she saw Philip's car at the warehouse. She considered hiding her car around the back of the building, knowing Philip would complain about her working on a Saturday. "And how do you know I was working on a Saturday? Were you working or were you stalking me?" Carina said to the empty hallway.

"Talking to yourself, Miss Whitley?" Philip leaned against his door jamb, arms folded, a wide grin on his face. "No, I'm not working, nor am I stalking you. Perhaps it's the other way around?"

"What are you doing here?" Carina asked. "Don't you have a strict 'no working on Saturday' policy?"

"Britney is rearranging my office," Philip moved aside. Britney was in the middle of the room, one hand on her hip, one tapping her chin.

Carina pulled her zippered sweatshirt closer. Her

ballet workout clothes were no match for Britney's designer jeans and short-sleeved cashmere sweater.

"Hello Carina," Britney said, without turning to look at her. "What do you think? Should I move the red one or leave it there?" She was staring at the large wall behind Philip's desk. Two abstract paintings adorned the wall. They were left over from the donated pieces Mr. Mansfield used to decorate his own office. Although these office spaces were temporary, they were tastefully decorated to inspire and give a glimpse of the artwork that would be part of the permanent collection.

Carina knew that Britney had some interior design experience, so she wisely deferred. "I'm no expert. I think I'd trust you to decide. From what Philip has told us, you have an excellent eye for design."

"Yes, I think I do," Britney said. "The red stays, I think. We'll have to do something with that atrocious statue, though."

"Nope," Philip said, lifting the maligned piece. The brass horse, a replica styled after a famous sculptor, wasn't an expensive or famous piece one would expect to see in a museum curator's office. "This was my grandfather's and it inspires me."

Britney pouted—a cute, photo-ready pout—and turned to Carina. "Help me out here?"

"I can't take sides," Carina said. "My favorite pieces are made by kindergartners, so I'm definitely not an expert." She wished them a fun afternoon and dropped her backpack in her office before heading to the storage area. The clean-up crew had left everything in the hallway, knowing she would need to reorganize it.

Half an hour later the couple stopped to say goodbye. "I saw your office, Carina," Britney asked. "Did you choose the pieces for the décor?" Carina glanced at Philip and back to Britney, unsure how to answer.

"Yes," she said. "I'm sure it could be improved, though."

"Au contraire," Britney said. "It was tasteful. You have a good eye."

"Thank you," she said, without pausing her box stacking. Friends had told her that when she felt strongly about something, her face broadcast it well, so she kept her head down. No value in Philip seeing that she wondered why he was still lingering around the office instead of showing his girlfriend around town. *Fiancée, not girlfriend,* she reminded herself, although she knew Philip stuck with the term *girlfriend.*

"You look like you have a full day ahead," Philip said as he handed her another box. "Do you need some help?"

Carina saw Britney's frown, and was sure the neighborhood heard the huff of disapproval. Well, the entire neighborhood except for Philip. Carina's quick thinking diffused the situation. "No, no, absolutely not! My carefully mapped-out schematic only makes sense to me. Go enjoy your day, you two." Turning back to her task, she missed the disappointment on Philip's face. Remembering her conversation with Mira, she warned herself. *He doesn't need rescuing.*

The task took less time than expected, thanks to the work she and the crew had done last night. Boxes were labeled and organized, and a spreadsheet hung on the storage closet wall. Being part of the ground floor of a new program meant she could organize in a way that made sense to her. So she made sure the decorations that could be used for any of the spring events were at the front of the space. Her need for practicality was sometimes obsessive, a trait tempered by time, but this time it proved helpful.

When she texted Philip to see when she might expect Britney to return, he responded quickly. *She'll be back late. She and some girlfriends are going out. She'll be leaving tomorrow.*

So, Carina had the rest of the afternoon and evening to herself. A long soak, newly painted nails, and a batch of brownies rounded out her day. She watched the last episode of her favorite comedy-filled crime drama before falling asleep. When a tipsy Britney returned close to midnight, Carina heard her on the phone with Philip, letting him know she was back at the apartment.

"Shhh, yourself, sir," she snapped at Philip. "I know she's asleep, duh."

Sunday morning Carina left the apartment early and was disappointed, but not surprised, to find Philip and Britney absent from church. His aunt's reaction was more pointed.

"Stop muttering, Emmie," Jay said. "He's a big boy and can make his own decisions."

"Bad ones," his wife said.

Snow flurries this far south were rare. Snow flurries that accumulated more than a dusting of snow were a bona fide phenomenon. True southerners panicked, northern transplants mocked. Philip waited for Carina in the apartment lobby. They had discussed the idea of carpooling, but decided against it since her schedule had to work around Mr. Mansfield's, which wasn't always consistent. Today he texted her before he left to offer her a ride, not sure if she was familiar with driving in wintry conditions.

She responded to his text. *Sure. On my way down. Thanks!* When she joined him, he helped her into her warm overcoat. She had paired a long jean skirt and boots with a teal green sweater. Philip bit back a groan. How could such down-to-earth clothes be more attractive than Britney's expensive, glamourous wardrobe?

"You look like this weather didn't catch you unprepared. Are you a secret northern transplant who has successfully adopted southern culture so well that no one knows your true identity?"

"Shh," she said, laughing as she buttoned her coat. "At one time you suspected I was a spy due to my expertise at disguises. Now you're dangerously close to ruining my cover."

On the way to the campus, Philip launched into interview code. He'd been filling the last slots for the project staff so it had become habit. Plus, he'd get some background information on Carina.

"All right, Miss Whitley, tell me about yourself. Where did you grow up? How many sisters and brothers? Why do you have a ready supply of winter clothes? Why do you seem to always be running to your next event or meeting or class?"

"College in the northeast, hence the winter clothes, and as you are aware, I like to keep busy," she said. "Remember? It keeps me out of trouble."

He noticed that she didn't answer all his questions. Family issues might be off-limits. Humor was his go-to in awkward situations, so he teased her instead of pushing her to answer. "You're still claiming it's meant to keep you out of trouble?" He laughed.

"How's that working out for you?"

"I'm sure you wouldn't want to compare trouble-making skills, sir. My schedule may in fact be part of my secret life, you know," she said. As they reached the office parking lot, she remembered a message she needed to deliver. "Speaking of schedules, are you on the church's singles group message loop? Did you hear about the ski retreat? It's not too late to sign up."

Philip appreciated Carina not mentioning that he had missed the announcement at church. His frustration with Britney was still fresh. His 'fiancée' had complained that her late afternoon flight was too early for her to risk going to church with him.

The snowball that hit him in the chest as he got out of his car snapped him out of his bad mood.

Years in the Chicago area gave Philip experience with snowball fights. After completing his Master of Art Administration he spent a few years there as an assistant curator. Of course, the snowfall in Illinois was considerably larger than the amount they'd received overnight. The layer of snow on the sidewalk was just enough to make a small ball to return fire. His shot missed—purposefully—and hit the column she had skirted behind. He bent down to make another as Tess pulled up. Carina laughed as he dropped it to cover his intentions.

Before going to his office, he followed Carina to hers. "Are you going?" he asked. "To the retreat?"

"Yes. I don't ski, but I like the scenery…and the company," she said. Over her shoulder she smiled as she added, "Or most of it."

"Funny," he said. "I'm putting in my registration today. Thanks for the reminder."

As students returned for the spring semester this week, Carina met with those assigned to work on the museum set up. Most were seniors majoring in Art History or Art Education, and she looked forward to getting their input on the community and children's programs. Mr. Mansfield's fundraising duties meant a quiet office for a couple of weeks. Carina caught up on paperwork, spreadsheets, and handwritten thank you notes for the donors. Finalizing choices for the grand opening promotional designs and the guest list for the fancy preliminary gala filled the rest of her work hours.

Except for an increased commitment to her ballet classes, her usual after-work activities lightened with the new semester. Other than trips to several art museums within driving distance and virtual tours of others, Carina searched for ways to stay busy some evenings. Rearranging her living room, clearing out kitchen cabinets, and a couple of visits to her small storage unit, succeeded in keeping her occupied. A welcome distraction came from Emilia.

Jay Lazlo insisted Emilia get out of the house. Now that her first trimester, and the terrible morning sickness, had passed, he knew she deserved a break. Her job as a part-time bank teller was flexible, but his wife tended to fill her time with caring for him and Sasha instead of treating herself to fun.

"He basically ordered me to relax," Emmie told Carina

when she called to invite her out for an evening. "We had a lively discussion about how ordering me to do something would not lend itself to a relaxing evening—for either him or me." She laughed. "Marriage is hilarious sometimes."

Carina suggested including Tess and Emilia agreed. They settled on an early dinner, a shopping trip to the new antique mall near the college, and dessert at Carina's. The evening was delightful. Emmie found a clock for the new baby's room, which was decorated in vintage artwork. Tess fell in love with a pair of antique earrings. The other two insisted on buying them to be Tess's 'something old' for her wedding.

While Emmie and Tess were debating on purchasing the matching necklace, Carina found a first edition of *The Count of Monte Cristo.* It was a little out of her price range, but she knew Philip collected them and she didn't remember seeing this one on his shelf. She'd make it a congratulations gift for the success of the project. Seeing that the other two were still shopping, she wandered into the children's toy section. She was fingering an intricate lace doll dress when Emmie joined her.

"That's pretty," she said, then saw the distress in her friend's eyes. "Oh, Carina, are you okay?"

Carina simply nodded, "Yes, sorry. I'm fine. Simply an unexpected memory." A quick topic change told Emmie that no more information would be forthcoming. "Did Tess decide on the necklace?"

"No, she's going to wait," Emmie said, letting Carina recover. "The necklace that went with the earrings was a little too elaborate for her dress. We're ready to go unless you want to keep shopping." Carina had purchased a salt and pepper shaker set for her Aunt Lynette. "My aunt collects them," she said. "I don't get to see her and my uncle often, but we're very close. They travel overseas regularly, but we have a family reunion every July and they are always in the county for Thanksgiving and Christmas."

A couple hours later, the smell of fresh brewed coffee and chocolate chip cookies, and lots of laughter filled Carina's apartment.

While they waited for the cookies to bake, Tess asked about the family photos on the fridge. "Are these your siblings, Carina?"

Photos from last year's July reunion, school pictures and artwork from her cousins' children, and an invitation to another cousin's wedding filled the door of Carina's refrigerator. "No, I'm an only child and so was my mom. My Aunt Lynette and Uncle Clark didn't have any children of their own. These are my aunt's nieces and nephews, but they always included us in their family gatherings, even before my parents passed." Carina paused as she fingered the photo of her parents. "So, yes, these guys are like my siblings. I talk to at least one of them every week and write letters to their kiddos. I'm looking forward to our July reunion. It's a highlight of my year."

Emmie filed away the information in her 'things Philip needs to know,' file. She had seen the spark of interest between him and Carina, but knew until he handled the Britney situation, she needed to protect him from further foolishness.

"I'm glad you live so far down the hallway from Philip," Emmie said as she put the last batch of cookies into the oven. "Growing up, he could smell my sister's baking from blocks away."

The ladies cleaned up the baking supplies, finishing as the oven timer beeped. Carina topped off their hot cocoa and after eating their fill of the warm cookies, they packed the rest of the cookies in a container to leave at Philip's door. Tess had an earlier day than the other two women, so she offered to drop the cookies and ring the doorbell. "It'll be fun. I haven't done a 'ring and run' in ages. The trick didn't fool him for long. Carina got a text within minutes. *"Where's the cold milk?"*

"I'm going to send him a link to the local grocery store," Carina said as she showed Emmie the text.

"Do it," his aunt said. They spent the next ten minutes in a text battle of the wits. Finally Emmie stepped in and called him. "Stop, Philip. Admit defeat. She's funnier than you."

"There, that should end the conversation," Emmie said. While she and Carina put away the remaining dishes, she asked about Britney's stay. "Did you get a chance to spend any time with her while she was here for the fundraiser?"

"She was out shopping or with Philip most of the time," Carina answered diplomatically. "I only saw her in passing in the mornings."

Emmie could hear that there was more to the story from her tone. "I was surprised she didn't push for Philip to let her stay with him, or beg for a hotel instead of a pull-out sofa." Seeing Carina bite her lip before turning away, Emmie pressed her. "She did sleep on the sofa, didn't she?" Carina's silence was answer enough.

"Please don't tell Philip," Carina said. "I know their relationship is tricky, and I don't want to make things worse."

"Like they could be any worse," Emmie mumbled. "Has he told you the story yet?"

"No."

"Well, he should," Emmie said. "A sense of honor is attractive, but infuriating sometimes."

Carina met Britney and Philip in the lobby of the apartment building the next afternoon after work. She was on her way to ballet practice, but arranged to meet them after Philip's frantic call that morning. Britney was back in town.

"Hello, Britney," Carina said. "I'm glad you were able to come for another visit. The fridge is stocked. Make yourself at home. You have my number if there's anything you need before I get home."

The frown on the gorgeous face caused Carina to hesitate. She glanced at Philip. He looked away.

"Let's get you settled, Britney," he said. "I'm sure you had a long day. Thanks, again, Carina."

Carina zipped up her duffle bag as they waited for the elevator, and the reason for Britney's displeasure became clear.

"You're such a fuddy-duddy, Philip," Britney said. "This isn't the Middle Ages. Why can't I stay in your apartment?" The elevator door closed before Philip answered, but not before he caught Carina's eye and she saw his irritation.

A text arrived within minutes. Whoever said you can't hear emotions through a text hadn't seen this one. Carina could hear Philip's voice. He'd discovered that Britney wasn't sleeping on Carina's pull-out sofa. The text was short, but she knew it wasn't the end of the conversation. *This is unacceptable. Why was I not informed?*

Britney's trip was unexpected, so Philip couldn't skip work the next morning to entertain her. Not that he was disappointed. An hour after his usual arrival time, Carina heard the elevator door. She suspected Philip's first topic of conversation would be the sleeping arrangements in her apartment and readied herself, arms crossed, as he reached her doorway.

"No, we will not discuss it. I offered, she accepted," Carina said. She didn't admit to switching the order of the offer and acceptance. In reality, Britney had settled into Carina's bedroom the night of the gala. She left Carina a note, not surprisingly short. *Thanks for the room. Your apartment is delightfully quaint.*

Carina was an instinctively caring person, but her short interactions with Britney were stretching even her long-suffering. How would Philip react if he knew her shower after ballet class last night had to wait until almost midnight? Britney's evening beauty routine was extensive.

"Please tell me that she behaved at least," he said as he read her mind. He slumped into the chair across from her desk when she didn't respond. "I texted her this morning and had to make a breakfast run. I hoped she'd sleep in, but apparently a need for a fresh cappuccino woke her."

He tapped the table with his notepad, not meeting Carina's gaze. Mr. Mansfield called him into the office, cutting short any chance that he'd press her to describe Britney's behavior. A large shipment of supplies was arriving today. The submissions from the campus were due by noon, also. Carina's duties included cataloging them, and she enjoyed perusing the artwork that had come in already. Although she didn't have an official vote on the selections, she definitely had favorites.

"Carina, please come here. We need you," Mr. Mansfield called through the open door. She grabbed a notepad and joined them.

"Thank you for the work you've done so far on the museum projects. I see we're ahead of schedule, which is good. I need Philip for some meetings today, so I'm asking if you can rearrange your schedule to entertain Miss Frost," Mr. Mansfield said. "She's a delightful young lady and we want to share our true southern hospitality."

Carina's heart sank, mainly because of the tasks still remaining, but also when she saw Philip's shoulder's droop. Her day now involved escorting Britney to several realty appointments. Philip's girlfriend—she had been asked not to refer to Britney as his fiancée—had plans for him to be in a home as soon as possible. Carina had overheard another heated conversation that morning, despite trying to avoid the couple as much as possible. "It's uncouth for the Head Curator of a museum to be living in a one bedroom designed for blue collar workers and college students," Britney had said. "What would your parents think?"

"They'd be proud of me," Philip said.

His comment raised more questions in Carina's mind. Emilia had talked about her sister and brother-in-law, mainly sharing funny stories of their times together. *This must be part of the 'long story' Philip promised to share at some point,* she thought.

Now her thoughts turned to today's duties. Philip and Mr. Mansfield laid out the day's new schedule. Philip would work through lunch on his tasks, and pulled a student worker in to accept the submissions that came in while Carina was away. She and Philip would switch places mid-afternoon and cataloging would begin. Carina agreed, and smiled through it all. No need to argue. Mr. Mansfield was a kind boss, but with the pressure of today's deadlines and deliveries, he missed her distress. Philip did not.

"Nice try, miss," Philip said as they left their boss's office. "You almost had me fooled. I know this change messes with your entire day. I'm so sorry. Will you be okay?" When she didn't answer immediately, he ran his fingers through his hair. It was a familiar habit, and one that Carina had seen several times when he was around Britney. "You know, this is ridiculous. I'm going to tell Britney she's on her own." He pulled out his phone, but Carina grabbed his arm before he could call her.

"No! I'm fine. I just have to make a call to change some plans tonight." When he didn't leave, she shooed him away. "Go. I'll be right behind you." He tarried long enough to hear part of her phone call. "I'm so sorry Mrs. Nelson. Can I meet with the twins tomorrow? I'll treat them to lunch while we study. If that doesn't work, can we do it after church on Sunday?"

Philip headed downstairs, not any less mad at Britney.

Tables outside the executive office were readied for the submissions. Carina joined him a few minutes later, and with both of them working, the set-up was done within a few minutes. The spreadsheet and registration forms were in place by the time the student chosen to help arrived. Martin, a senior art marketing student, was one of Carina's favorites. A hard worker and talented artist himself, he was thankful to be pulled off the work at the warehouse.

"I'll be back before your afternoon class, Martin," she said. "Hopefully, there will be a steady flow and not an onslaught at noon. Thank you so much. You're a gem!"

"No problem, Ree," he said. "I hope the emergency isn't anything too tragic."

Carina glanced at Philip, eyebrow raised. "No, not too tragic," she said, adding as she passed Philip, "at least I hope not."

Chapter 7
I'll make this up to you

In many states, any experience or education in Interior Design qualified you to work in the field. Some required a license to use the title Interior Designer, informing clients that you had the education to back your work. Britney had a natural eye for design, and carried business cards listing herself as an Interior Designer. Carina suspected, but didn't confirm, that a bachelor's degree, or even state certification, wasn't something Britney had pursued. Her questions were answered as her talkative companion prefaced several of her critical takes on a homeowner's paint scheme, artwork placement, or kitchen countertop choices, with "I'm not a *certified* designer, but surely *anyone* can see that this is wrong." She alternated between 'wrong,' 'hideous,' and 'a crime against design,' as they trudged through five or six different homes. Carina was so exhausted, she'd lost count.

A call at two o'clock was Carina's salvation.

"Yes, Philip," Britney purred. "I know she has to get back to work." She pointed to the phone and shook her head. "Men. But what can you do?"

On their way back to the office, Britney made a list

of her likes and dislikes. Not surprisingly the latter was longer. *Poor Philip,* Carina thought, then mentally apologized and prayed for patience. *Lord, help me show mercy and grace to this woman. Thank you for protecting my words.*

As they parked, Britney smiled and revealed her masterplan. It was for Carina to be Philip's guide since he now would have to look for property on his own. "I'll finish this list and send it to you," Britney said. "I know you'll do me proud."

Carina cringed, but the clock on the dashboard reminded her that she had to hurry. She scrambled from the car when she saw Philip waiting, dialing the campus pizza shop next door so she didn't stop to talk. Being mid-afternoon meant they had her small pizza ready by the time she completed her payment and grabbed her soda.

Still behind schedule, she passed Philip and Britney as she got off the elevator. "Here, Britney," Philip handed her his keys, "go on down. I want to check in with Carina before I leave." He put his girlfriend on the elevator and pressed the down button before she could object. Seeing Carina's carryout bag and soda, he followed her to the break room. "You two didn't have lunch?"

A shake of her head was all Carina offered as she gulped down a slice of pizza. Breakfast had been a single piece of toast since Britney snuck into the bathroom before she did, effectively upending her morning routine. Carina was only able to brush her teeth and swipe some mascara on her lashes in order to make it to work without being late.

Philip reached across the table and wiped a spot of tomato sauce that had missed her mouth. "I promise I'll make this up to you."

The tours of endless homes in high heels produced an aching back, and even with working the rest of the afternoon and evening barefoot, Carina was in pain by the time she got home. A scribbled note from Philip on her kitchen counter let her know he and Britney would be out for the rest of the evening. It was after nine o'clock, but she took the chance that 'the rest of the evening' gave her enough time for a soak in the bathtub. It did, but her exhaustion was so deep that wrapping her hair in a towel and pulling on her most comfortable pjs was all she could manage before hunger competed with fatigue. Promising herself she'd eat the rest of her pizza and dry her hair later was a plan unfulfilled.

A sleeping co-worker, half-eaten pizza and rolling credits from a romantic comedy greeted Philip as he opened the door at midnight. Britney disregarded her slumbering hostess as she dropped her purse loudly on the coffee table. Philip turned on her and pointed her to the bedroom. "Go to bed, Britney. You have an early flight tomorrow. Goodnight."

He cleaned up the meal and turned off the TV, allowing Carina time to gather herself. She made it to the bathroom before Britney claimed it, combed out her hair and braided it. When she rejoined Philip in the kitchen he apologized for his girlfriend…again.

"It's okay, Philip, honestly," Carina said. "Go get some sleep."

"Carina," he said. He reached for her hand and started to move closer, until he saw her pale. He dropped his arm and stepped back. "Thank you again. Goodnight."

Sunday morning Philip slid into the pew across from Emmie, leaned forward and waved to Sassy who was sitting between her mom and Carina. He paused, hoping Carina would look his way. She didn't. The music started and Philip turned his thoughts to the service. He knew he needed to tell Carina the truth, sooner rather than later.

As the congregation cleared out, Philip texted Carina, asking her to meet him in the parking lot. He watched to see if she looked at her phone but she was surrounded by friends from the singles class. Jay, a firefighter, was called in to work late last night to cover a co-worker's shift, so Philip walked Emmie and Sasha to the car, keeping an eye out for Carina. His patience paid off and he intercepted her path to her car. "Good morning, Miss Whitley."

Carina glanced at her watch and corrected him. "Good *afternoon* Mr. Corelli."

Philip relaxed. She either had forgiven him for the awkwardness of Friday night, or was willing to pretend she had. Never one for small talk, he skipped the informal conversation and jumped in the deep end. "Have you forgiven me?"

"For what?" she asked, but didn't turn away quick enough to hide her grin. "There are so many possibilities."

"Pick one," he said, helping her with the bags she'd acquired somewhere between the end of the service and the parking lot. "What's all this stuff?"

"All this *stuff* is a donation of art supplies for the museum. You know—that project the college is working on—perhaps you've heard of it?"

"Wow, Carina," he said. "Why this levity? I was prepared for a tongue-lashing." He paused as she arranged the bags so they wouldn't spill their contents, likely including jars of glitter, in her backseat. "Not that I don't deserve it."

"We both know Friday was not your fault, so I think we shouldn't mention it again."

He followed her around to the driver's side, knowing that for him, the Friday night misstep didn't involve Britney at all. Now he had to decide how to ask what he needed to, and not what he wanted to.

"Since you seem to be the bigger person here, I have a favor to ask," he said. "More like beg, plead, bribe if necessary."

Carina turned and stared at him, pausing long enough for him to squirm. "You need me to look at houses for you," she said.

Philip's mouth opened but no words emerged. He tried again. Still nothing. *How did she do that?*

Moments passed until she took pity on him. "Britney asked me before she left yesterday. She says I know what she likes, and won't let you talk me into anything that wouldn't win her approval."

"She didn't." Philip saw his future life flash before his eyes. Dread was all he could feel. Carina's smile brought him back to hope.

"Yes, and I told her I'd love to," Carina said.

"Honestly, except for doing it in high heels, I enjoyed the house hunting, even though we didn't find anything suitable. I think I have a good idea of what she wants."

Any casual observer would have seen the unspoken message that passed between them. *'What she wants.'* They both knew it was more than a house.

Friday night dinner was a regular event for Philip and the Lazlos. When he arrived with the pizzas, he was disappointed to see that Carina hadn't accepted their invitation. "She said something about catching up on some work," Emmie said. "Are you guys working her too hard? I wish she caught up on some rest instead. Did you know there are a ton of activities other than work that she's involved in?" Carina's defender listed her extra-curricular activities with the zeal of a public defender. Tutoring, volunteering at the gift shop during her lunch time, classes at a local gym , and the side project for the museum, were the ones Emilia knew of. "I suspect there are others," she said. "She seems to have an insatiable need to stay occupied."

Her normally talkative nephew let Sasha climb on him without the usual make-believe tale of a magical squirrel or rabbit or baby bird scurrying up a tree or castle wall or mountain. Even the four-year old noticed. "Uncle Philip, you're not telling the story!"

He shook himself out of the malaise and complied. Sasha didn't seem to mind that the story was shorter and less fantastical than usual. Her dad interpreted his wife's look, and rescued Philip. "Nap time, Miss Polka-dot Giraffe. Let's let the Pineapple tree rest." Philip's tales were always entertaining.

Jay joined his wife and Philip a few minutes later. The conversation was solemn. "You need to tell Carina the whole story," Jay said. "She deserves to know, especially if she's putting up with some of Britney's antics." His wife shook her head. "You don't agree, Em?"

"I'm torn," she said. "I'd love to tell her, but I know I'd not be as kind or merciful as needed." Britney was not on her list of favorite people, or even those she tolerated. "But, Philip," she said, squeezing his arm, "be careful. I see the way you are with Carina. You are not free to follow the feelings you're beginning to entertain."

Philip nodded. "Pray for me. I'll do my best to not make Britney look worse than she manages to do all by herself." At the raised eyebrow from his 'Uncle Jay' he winced. "Sorry. I'm trying."

He sent Carina a text, asking her to meet him at the coffee shop around the corner from their apartment building. A public space was safer.

Chapter 8
Thank you for trusting me

Conversations at work over coffee versus tea and latte versus espresso, meant that Philip knew what to get for Carina. He added two pieces of pie to the order and waited for her to arrive.

What to tell her without further tarnishing Britney's character? How to preserve their friendship and avoid the temptation to hope for something deeper?

Carina arrived while he stared at his coffee. "Wake up, Mister." She said as she unwound her scarf that she had grabbed after checking the weather report. "Is that decaf or are you daydreaming?"

"Carina. Thanks for meeting me." He stood and helped her out of her coat. "We need to talk."

She waited as Philip rearranged the silverware on the table, twice, before he shoved a hand through his hair and took a deep breath.

"It was six months ago," he said. "I had fulfilled my contract at the museum there, and decided to put out feelers for a change. Britney's father was on the board and put me in contact with several opportunities, including this project championed by the Mansfield family. I had no idea how much my life was about to change."

"Philip, you don't have to explain anything to me," Carina said, squeezing his arm. "But if you need to talk about it, I'll listen." When he didn't relax, she tried a bit of humor. "Even if this is going to be a long story like you promise."

The Corelli's lived a modest life that confused those that knew of the family's wealth. It was substantial, but most of it funded charities. Philip's grandfather believed giving children money without demanding responsibility was not good parenting.

"I was at a low point in my faith," Philip explained. "Making bad decisions, unhappy in my job, unsure about my future." He fell silent and Carina didn't push him. She offered a bite of her apple pie, since he had ordered cherry, and he reciprocated. They laughed when they both preferred the other's pie, and proceeded to clean their plates. "Preferences noted," Philip said.

After the waitress cleared their plates, he continued his story. They met at a fundraiser for the museum. Her father introduced them and their first date was the next night. "She was beautiful, I was vulnerable, but that's no excuse."

Britney was charming and Philip missed the initial red flags. By their third date, her conversation turned to his family, his upbringing, and questions about what it was like to grow up in such a well-known family.

Philip saw Carina's eyes widen. "Yup, I should've known, but well," he said with a shrug, "I'm a guy." The waitress stopped to see if they needed anything. They ordered a plate of cheese fries and shared it while he finished his story.

Britney didn't believe Philip when he explained that he didn't have a huge trust fund, nor did he want one. She thought he was playing hard to get. "Then a call from my lovely Aunt Emilia changed everything," he said. He remembered the conversation well.

"You've been on our mind lately, nephew," she had said. "Anything going on?" The Lazlos had been praying for him and when he told them about Britney, Emmie's familial psychic powers appeared. "Tell me more, Philip. What's she like? Does she go to your church?"

"She asked you that?" Carina interrupted. "Sounds exactly like something Emilia Lazlo would do."

"Yes. Yes, she did," he said. "I ignored the question and described how much fun we'd been having, how pretty she was, and how much help her dad had given me in looking for another job."

"Did she buy that?" Carina offered him the last bite of her pie.

"Nope. She didn't push me, but definitely made me realize I needed to evaluate my life and choices. Still, I thought Britney would be part of those choices," he said, "just not this big a part." He checked his watch and realized they had talked for almost an hour. "Almost done, I promise," he said.

When Britney turned down his invitation to join him at church on Sunday, he grew concerned. The scripture readings from Proverbs convicted him, especially those warning against being influenced by people that lead you away from your faith. "I kept hearing the pastor talk about those that 'care nothing about the path of life,' and I knew I had to end it with Britney," he explained.

When he told Brittney his decision, her tears seemed genuine. He hesitated and agreed to give the relationship another chance. A week later, a late-night party and a girlfriend that drank too much, ended in a seemingly compromising situation.

Philip watched for Carina's reaction, but only saw concern. "Nothing happened, I promise, but Britney left out important details when she told her father." Philip Corelli and Britney Frost were unofficially engaged the next day.

"I'm so sorry, Philip," Carina said. "Thank you for trusting me." She hesitated. "Is there anything I can do?"

"She's not a terrible person," he said. "I've since realized the pressure comes partly from her parents, but her lack of interest in sharing my faith is my biggest concern," he said. "I can't keep going like this. Every second I spend with her I find myself getting more annoyed."

Carina grabbed the bill and stood. "Let's walk," she said and headed to the cashier before he could stop her. Outside they headed to a nearby park that had acres of pathways featuring colorful flowers during spring and summer and unusual art installations year-round. They walked in silence for several minutes, until they found a trail featuring evergreen topiaries, and discussed possibly pursuing a partnership with the park to promote the museum. Finally, they spotted a secluded bench along a path away from the other park visitors.

"Philip," Carina said, "My advice probably won't be what you want to hear, but I'm going to give it anyway. I learned a long time ago to speak up when I see someone I care about struggling."

Philip swallowed the lump in his throat. "Bring it on."

"Lean in, Philip," she said. "I know it may feel like pretending, but try to give her your best effort. Treat her like you care about her, which I know you do on some level."

When he didn't respond, she continued. "You need to trust that God has a reason for letting you go through this. We need to trust He will guard you and guide you. Your faith is important, and your actions should show that." Silence still from Philip. "Maybe this is for her sake? To show her the peace and contentment that faith can bring. We should be praying for her and for you."

He stood and turned away. "You're right." His voice revealed a depth of emotions. Carina reached for his hand. He turned back and pulled her to her feet. "Thank you, my friend. I think I need to spend some time alone. Will you make it safely out of the park and back home?"

She gave him a quick hug and promised to text him when she arrived. "I'll be praying for you."

He walked the park for almost an hour, praying. Some walkers looked confused as they passed him, but 'praying with your eyes open,' was a concept his father had encouraged in his children. Jokingly, when they learned to drive they often teased him. "Don't worry, Dad. We'll be praying with our eyes open on the way to school."

Over the years Philip had found that using this spiritual device helped his prayer life. Commuting times now involved praying for the community, the emergency vehicles and those they were rushing to help, gratefulness for a job he loved, and an appreciation for sunrises and sunsets. Today his prayers were fervent, but the beauty of the park calmed him. He knew he was at a crossroads.

Father, thank you for the beauty of your creation and the comfort it brings. Thank you for family and friends that hold me accountable. Please help me honor you and my faith in my relationship with Britney. Help me trust you and your plans for me. Calm my fears and guard my attitude, as I try to show her the importance of my relationship with you.

Museum construction wrapped up the next week, but Philip's duties increased. Decisions about which pieces to display, research to do for descriptions for the exhibition guide, hiring photographers, and assigning art students to inspect all the pieces stretched his management and planning skills. Mr. Mansfield busied himself attending lunches with donors and keeping the board members updated. His absence freed Philip's schedule, and he knew Carina's productivity benefitted. Their boss was a delightful man, but his penchant for story telling hampered progress at this crucial phase of the project.

Philip glanced at his watch and knew the gift shop was closing soon. Carina mentioned in passing that she was helping Tess unpack a delivery today. *Helping was enough of an excuse to stop by, right?*

Carina had finished her work early so she could help Tess. As they unpacked the boxes, Tess mentioned the delivery of frames for the opening. "Philip said you were reframing some of the Mansfield collection. Are they in bad shape?"

"Some, but not all," she said. "A few of the pieces

81

were bought from a collector that, in my opinion, hadn't understood the importance of the frame."

Like a guilty child, Philip had heard his name from the door of the shop. He hid and eavesdropped. *I'll apologize later.*

Much of what Carina explained to Tess, he knew from his various courses. Still it was fascinating to hear her add layers to his own understanding.

"A gilded frame automatically conveys wealth and opulence, often distracting from the simplicity, peacefulness, or mood of the actual artwork. I've sometimes researched what an artist said about a particular work—the message he wanted to send, why he painted the piece, the time period, etc. If a frame takes away from that, it dishonors the artist."

She added that good framing adds value, changes the observer's perceptions, sets a mood. "It's not too different from how we frame ourselves."

"Ah," Tess replied. "Like a fancy outfit making you think someone is worth knowing, until you find out it's not necessarily true."

"Yes," Carina said, adding, "and the opposite is true. Simple clothing, even rags, sometimes hides the kindest souls." The pair fell silent as they unpacked the last few boxes.

Philip almost left, but was glad he didn't as he heard Carina's last comment, "God often reframes our lives, our pasts, our hurts, our mistakes, which changes our perspective, our self-esteem, our outlook," she said, "and reminds us that He values us so very much."

Lord, this young woman has my heart. Help me be wise. Philip slipped out before Tess came to lock up.

Two days later Carina was scheduled to substitute in the gift shop. Philip stopped in at the end of the normal lunch hour. Since students were back on campus the textbook section, closed off after the break, now doubled the size of the store. He snaked his way through the aisles, dodging students trying to get souvenirs for the weekend's big basketball game. When he finally made it to the cashier line, Tess greeted him, leaning around the line of shoppers in front of her. "She's already gone," she said before he could ask. He saluted his thanks and decided now was a perfect time to collect the blueprints from Mr. Mansfield's office that he wouldn't actually need until tomorrow.

Because of the crowds, Carina and Tess had both worked through the lunch rush. Carina promised to come back mid-afternoon to give Tess a break. With a few minutes to spare before her own lunch hour was over, Carina found a quiet corner around the corner from her office. She kicked off her shoes and sank into a padded armchair, legs dangling over the side. While sipping her smoothie—the only meal the short timeframe allowed—she decided to call her aunt and uncle.

"How's Italy? I'll bet the food is beyond fabulous," she said. "I'm sure it's better than this..." she wrinkled her nose as she showed them her drink, "...banana strawberry smoothie."

"That sounds delicious," Philip said as he came around the corner. "You look comfortable." Seeing he'd interrupted a conversation he stopped and started to back up.

"Philip, come," Carina said. "Meet my family. This is

my Aunt Lynette and Uncle Clark."

He pulled a side table over and sat down behind her, greeting her guardians over her shoulder. "Mr. and Mrs. Whitley, so nice to meet you. You'll be glad to know Carina is behaving...for the most part." He dodged Carina's elbow.

"This is Philip," she said, "and as you can see, he's not behaving, but that's not unusual."

They talked for almost ten minutes, discussing both the headaches and payoffs of international travel. "The artwork experience alone is worth the effort," Mr. Whitley said.

"Where are you heading next?" Philip asked.

"We're going to Turin, Italy," Lynette Whitley said. "It's mentioned in one of my favorite novels and I've always wanted to visit."

"Ah, yes," said Philip. "From *Around the World in Eighty Days*? It's one of my favorites. I have a first edition I found at an antique store in Chicago."

"Yes," Mrs. Whitley said. "I have a life goal of doing a shorter version of the trip someday. Maybe around the world in eight weeks."

"Sounds wonderful," Philips said as noise from the stairwell indicated the returning students. He realized he'd monopolized their conversation. "I'm sorry for interrupting your call. Thank you for raising such a wonderful young lady."

"It was easy," Lynette Whitley said, "and so nice to finally meet you."

Carina caught Philip's raised eyebrow and knew he'd tease her later about her aunt's 'finally meet you' statement. The lateness of the time allowed her to escape any further questioning. Pointing to her watch, she said her goodbyes. "I'll talk to you after the retreat. I love you!"

As expected, Philip was waiting at her desk. "So, you've told them about me," he said. "All the good parts, right?"

"What good parts?" Carina asked.

He clutched his chest. "Ouch, seriously? I may never recover," he said. "They seem nice. It's great that they can travel so much. Were you ever able to go with them?" His back was turned as he unlocked Mr. Mansfield's door to retrieve a set of blueprints needed at the warehouse. When he turned he saw Carina's frown only seconds before she hid it.

"Yes, it was marvelous," she said, a bright smile firmly in place.

He let the boss's door close and stepped back toward Carina. "Not as marvelous as your smile implies, I gather. What's up?"

"Nothing," she said, "or at least nothing for you to worry about."

Philip ignored her dismissal and sat on the edge of her desk. "Nope. Tell me." When she ignored him in return, he softened his approach. "Please, please, please? You know my sordid Britney story. I won't pressure you, but you know I can be trusted," he said. "And I care."

"I'm fine, honestly," she said. "It's only latent guilt that raises its head occasionally." Her family traveled often. Business dealings took her uncle overseas every few months and now that her aunt retired from teaching, which she waited to do until Carina graduated from college, she joined him. Philip knew her parents had died when she was a child, so she didn't have to explain why her aunt and uncle raised her. "As a preteen, I loved the summer trips. We visited castles and art museums, ate delicious foods, and bungled all sorts of languages." She turned to move stacks around the table behind her desk. Her pause stretched out.

"Carina, you don't have to share anything you don't want to," Philip said. "I shouldn't have pressured you. I'll grab the files I need and leave you to get your work done."

"No, wait," she said. "I'll explain. As a young child, it never occurred to me that my aunt and uncle had a life before me. I figured that out when I was older."

When she was fifteen she uncovered a letter from her mom to her aunt. Her parents were writing a will, a task they had put off far too long—and one that turned out to be timely. "I memorized part of the letter. 'We know it would be a huge sacrifice, but you are the only ones we trust to raise Carina in a godly, loving home, if anything should happen to us.' When it did, my aunt and uncle dropped everything and came to get me as soon as they could."

Up to that point Lynette Whitley had been an online instructor, able to conduct class from anywhere. She'd moved into a traditional classroom when they'd gained custody of Carina, and her uncle took a different position in his company so they traveled less until Carina was older.

"When my parents died, their life changed

drastically," she said. "Now you can pretend to be my uncle and remind me that I shouldn't feel guilty."

"I'm not your uncle, but I agree with his wisdom," he said. "I know you, Carina. If Emilia and Jay had no other family, and asked you to be Sassy's guardian, you wouldn't blink an eye." He had moved to her side while she told her story. He tilted her chin up. "You reflect the wonderful family that raised you. They are right to tell you to let go of the guilt. Trust that you were always in your heavenly father's hand."

"Thank you," she said, her tone more abrupt than he'd hoped, but he decided he'd pushed her enough, so he stepped back.

"I'll be out of your way in a minute," he said. "I know you're getting a lot done this week, and I, too, have made good progress. I think our boss will be pleased when he gets back." He stopped again after locking Mr. Mansfield's door. "Call me if you need anything."

Carina smiled and nodded.

Chapter 9
What other talents are you hiding?

Keeping his promise to change his relationship with Britney would be harder than expected. Nightly conversations didn't always end well. Britney complained about her parents' insistence that she look for a job. She was frustrated that his parents hadn't spread the word of their engagement on their numerous social media platforms. Several times the calls ended with her telling him that he was settling for so much less than he deserved as a Corelli. Philip battled responding to this obvious ploy to confirm his family's wealth. He'd run out of phrases to use to explain his situation. *I am not rich, nor do I want to be.* Her latest complaint was about his not finding them a house yet. Philip prayed for patience and help changing his yearnings. Right now finding a house to share with Britney was not appealing. "Have Carina find us a house," Britney said. "Perhaps she'll have more luck. She hangs out with Grayson, so he can help, too. I'm sure *he's* got good taste. How could he be part of the Mansfield Family and not, right?"

"Right. I'll ask her," Philip had answered. "Goodnight, my dear," he forced himself to say. *Lean in,* he heard Carina's words in his head. *"I'm trying, Lord,"* he prayed.

True to her earlier offer, Carina agreed to help by going with Philip to look at more homes. They both nixed the idea of Grayson joining them. Encouraging interaction between Grayson and Britney didn't seem wise. The night of the fundraising banquet, Grayson's father had quizzed Carina about Britney. Grayson told her later that his father had done a deep dive into Britney's social media postings. "I'm supposed to stay away from her," he had told Carina.

Britney sent a list of additional houses for them to inspect. All but a few were out of Philip's price range. His realtor provided another list and their first outing was planned. They were going to look at two houses that appeared on both lists. The first one was a modern, sophisticated home with white carpets, white walls, white tile, and white countertops in the kitchen. While Carina took notes and photos, Philip and the realtor went over the details. Standing in the living room, looking toward the kitchen, Philip could imagine the damage that a toddler could do with a house that was basically a blank white canvas. For a moment, his heart sank. Imagining children with Britney was frightening. The realtor's phone ringing snapped him out of his mood.

"I have a closing that is running into some issues," the realtor said as he locked the key box. "I'll have my new assistant meet you at the next house, if that's okay?" Philip thanked him for his help and promised to check in after they looked at the second property.

When Carina came downstairs she said, "The master bath is too small. Britney has that number three on her list." They discussed the rest of the pros and cons as they drove to the next house.

"If this was my list, there'd be more cons than pros for that place," Philip muttered. He glanced at Carina and saw her shake her head. "Sorry. I am trying."

A Victorian exterior and beautiful landscaping made the next house look more expensive than the listing price. It was smaller than the square footage Britney had on her list, and the neighborhood wasn't the upscale one at the top of the list. Hopefully, the interior would be acceptable.

They were looking at the details of the listing when a red sportscar zipped into the driveway. The young realty agent hopped out and greeted them. "Hey guys! Let's look at this beauty!" Carina and Philip shared a look, part humor, part concern.

The listing requested that they take off their shoes, not an unusual requirement if the homeowners had recently replaced the carpet. As planned, Carina went upstairs to look at the extra bedrooms, while Philip and the agent checked out the master suite, dining room, and kitchen. They planned to meet back in the living room. The men were looking at the kitchen while they waited for Carina, who had called down from the upstairs loft saying she'd be there in a minute.

A low whistle caught Philip's attention. The young realty assistant stood in the kitchen doorway watching Carina take photos of the living room from the upstairs loft. "Wow," he said as Philip joined him. "She's not bad."

"Excuse me?" Philip said. The clueless young man

turned back into the kitchen.

"Your friend there," he said. "Hey, she's barefoot and we're in the kitchen. I'll flip you for the pregnant part." The words were barely out of his mouth before he found himself backed into the pantry door.

Philip took a couple deep breaths. Punctuating his words with a firm finger in the man's chest, he issued an ultimatum. "I should have you slammed against the wall right now, but I'll settle for your immediate departure. You might also consider an out-of-town move, because your boss will be receiving a call from me this afternoon describing your offensive ignorance." The man was backing his car out of the driveway less than a minute later.

"Where's the realtor?" Carina asked when she reached the kitchen.

"He was called away," Philip said, "but said we could take our time and lock up when we're done. I'm going to check out the backyard while you take the photos down here. We can compare notes later."

She finished the photos, then spied the bay window seat overlooking the backyard. She nestled into the spot to make notes on all the details of the house. It was so different from the last one, and satisfied very few of Britney's wishes. Carina whispered to the empty room, "For me, though, it's wonderful." She glanced out the window and saw that Philip was on the phone, probably with Britney, so she explored the rest of the downstairs. In the foyer she found the sound system that piped music throughout the home. Selecting the menu option marked 'Classical,' she smiled as the room filled with

Tchaikovsky. Making sure Philip was still occupied, she danced across the room, executing a pirouette, arabesque, and a few jumps. Caught up in the music, she lost track of time. As she bowed to the invisible audience, she saw Philip. He was leaning against the arched doorway that led to the master suite.

"Ballet, Miss Whitley?" He asked as he applauded her. "What other talents are you hiding from me?"

Carina glanced up from her reverence position. "Too many to count." He pushed away from the wall and offered his hand.

"So, this house is perfect for Britney, wouldn't you say?" He asked.

"Most definitely," she said, mirroring his satirical tone. "I'll call her right now if you like."

"You're hilarious," he said. "I see that stand-up comedy is also a gift. Honestly, what do you think of this one?"

"I love the old charm matched with the modern conveniences," Carina said, "but the first one we saw meets more of her standards. Remind me, though, to check if this one's available when I'm ready to buy…you know, when I win the lottery."

"You play the lottery?" Philip asked.

"No," she laughed, "but one can always dream."

On their way back to the office, Carina asked Philip how his commitment to wooing Britney was working. "Honestly, Philip," she said, "is she responding at all?"

"Sort of," he said, "but wait, 'wooing Britney'? Is that the best you've got? I thought you were a spy, remember? At least at our first meeting you were a master of disguise, and since then I've seen the numerous comings-and-goings of your mysterious after-hours activities. Surely you could come up with a better code name for my little project."

"True," she said. "How about 'Grace for Britney,' or 'Brit-demption'?"

Philip groaned. "Since it's my attitude change that's the objective, what about 'Thawsville' since my heart was so hard? Or 'Eyes Open,' or even better 'Eyes Closed'?" He grinned when he saw her frown. "I'm kidding."

"So, 'Wooing Britney' it is," Carina said. "You said she's 'sort of' responding? What did you mean?"

Philip described the lack of response Britney had given when he started his campaign a couple of weeks ago. Since, she'd become alternately more frustrating and less communicative. He suspected she was losing interest. "That's not simply wishful thinking, either" he said before Carina reacted. "Honestly, she's stopped mentioning my family's money, and I had to beg her to send me this list of houses."

"I won't go so far as to say that's good news," Carina said, "but we were praying for answers. It's going to work out, Philip. Keep trusting."

"I'm working on that," he said. "Thanks for your help—all of it." Carina waved as she headed upstairs. He needed to get to the warehouse, but stared after her long after she disappeared inside the building. *Lord, help me.*

Chapter 10
Be careful and behave

The weather cooperated with the church's ski retreat plans. The group message chain filled with reports of ideal snow conditions. Philip stopped by Carina's office before heading home to pack. They had decided to carpool to the church, but her plans had changed when she overheard a conversation between Grayson and Mr. Mansfield.

"She said it would be lame, and now she's not going," Grayson had said. Carina suspected the 'she' was Britney. She had seen Britney's name on Grayson's phone one day when he had misplaced it in the office. "No way I'm giving up a weekend of skiing for anyone, not even her."

Her frustrated boss grumbled loud enough for Carina to hear from her desk. Mr. Mansfield was one of the calmest men she knew. Grayson's behavior had improved over the last few weeks, but the constant need for supervision was tiring. Carina empathized.

"Aren't you supposed to be staying away from her anyway?" His uncle said as Grayson started to leave.

"Oh, yeah," the young man said. "You're right. So this is good."

Deciding not to reveal her accidental eavesdropping,

she told Philip, "Grayson's changed his mind, again. I'll ride with him if that's ok. I need to school him a bit on the atmosphere of the retreat. He seems to be open to the spiritual talks we've had, which aren't many, but it's been encouraging. I know the group will be patient with him, too."

"Sounds good," Philip said. Carina knew him well enough to sense his disappointment, but wasn't sure if it was because of her or because Britney had suddenly had a pressing engagement that couldn't be changed. "Ironic choice of words," Philip had said when he told Carina that morning.

Grayson spent most of the four-hour bus ride on his phone, scrolling through social media, and playing games. Carina was on the aisle of the bus, so she was able to converse with Philip, Tess, and Lincoln who were in adjacent seats. When they arrived at the chalet, some of the group headed straight to the slopes. The night skiing was optional and before she backed out of the trip, Britney had complained that she'd be tired, so Philip hadn't signed up for the session. Grayson had, so Carina had the evening to herself.

The chalet was a three-story Tudor style building. The rooms had bunk beds, but these were not the rustic, uncomfortable type familiar to anyone who had attended summer camp as a child. The polished pine wood and rich decoration gave a sense of rustic elegance. The kitchen and large living room was on the ground floor which featured a large stone fireplace, a pool table, and a wide screen television. It was obvious they wouldn't be roughing it this weekend.

After everyone settled in their rooms, the leaders set out a late snack and asked everyone to sign up for a turn helping with the meals. Philip and Carina chose Sunday's breakfast. She penciled in Grayson's name, too. There were boxes of meal supplies and suitcases in the bus that needed to be unloaded, so he joined the volunteers. Since the rooms were all upstairs, some of the men carried the suitcases to the second-floor landing so individuals could put them in their chosen rooms.

When Philip joined the group in the open living area, he spotted Carina prepping the meal in the kitchen. The sign-up sheet was on the fridge and he pointed to it, eyebrow raised.

"Miss Whitley," he said as he helped her pour chips into bowls, "I see your name is not on the list for tonight's meal preparation. Perhaps you can explain why you are here and not enjoying the roaring fire and scintillating conversation in the other room."

Carina laughed. "Since I saw you arrive downstairs minutes ago, how could you know that the conversation is scintillating? And perhaps I'm hungry and wanted first dibs on these goodies," she said as continued chopping onions for the pico de gallo. When she wiped her eyes, Philip turned her to face him.

"It's only been an hour since we arrived. Did you miss me so much that you're in tears?"

"Of course," she said, accepting the napkin he handed her. "I'm using the onions to cover my despair."

"Good. I was afraid you-know-who had done something to upset you and I'd have to have a word with him."

Carina had been honest enough with Philip about her arrangement with Grayson, that she felt free to comment, although she did so in a whisper. "I'd have to be more emotionally involved for you-know-who to upset me," she said. "Although I do need to have a conversation with him. His uncle will want a debrief on Monday and right now I'm not sure how to grade him. I asked him to come help in the kitchen before he left for the night run, and he said, 'nice try, sweetheart.' I almost punched him."

Philip choked. He had just taken a sip of coffee and now Carina was pounding his back. "I would've paid money to see that." He lingered in the kitchen, unloading and organizing the supplies he'd helped bring in, but out of the way of the snack makers.

When Carina took the fresh-baked chocolate chip cookies off the baking pan, she swatted his hand away as he tried to steal one. "Stop it. These are hot."

"C'mon, Carina," he said as he ignored her and grabbed one from the cooling rack. "I'll bet you've never stolen a cookie from the cookie jar."

"I'm not an angel, Philip," she said. To prove it, she popped one of the large gooey goodies into her mouth.

"Are you enjoying yourself? Do you look forward to skiing? Are you glad Grayson went on the night run?" He peppered her questions, grinning as she glared at him. "How's the cookie? Bigger and richer than expected?" She nodded and he poured her a glass of milk.

"Thank you," she said, once she'd recovered. "Yes, no, and no comment." When he looked confused, she clarified. "Yes I'm enjoying myself, or at least I was until I almost choked, no I don't like skiing, and yes, my happiness is not tied to Grayson Mansfield."

"Hey Ree! Philip!" A call from the living room ended

their banter. "We need another couple for the game." Philip saw the blush Carina tried to hide. Hopefully the 'couple' label was unintentional. He'd vowed to guard his actions. They joined the group for a rousing and hilarious guessing game using Tess's phone. The oven buzzer sounded, signaling the next batch of cookies was ready. Philip settled next to Carina as the others headed to the snacks.

"Don't you want another cookie?"

"Hush," she said. "You're not funny."

"Au contraire," he said. "I've been told I'm hilarious...by you, if I remember correctly."

Carina shook her head. "I remember others saying you were hilarious, and I also remember you admiring my sense of humor which you said helped my stand-up comedy career."

He acquiesced and offered to get them both a cup of hot chocolate, returning with a plate of snacks to share. The group had quieted and many were involved in smaller conversations.

"You don't ski?" Philip circled back to their previous conversation. "Why? Do you want to try?"

"No. I'm fine."

"Are you afraid?"

"Not particularly," she said, "but I don't agree with the premise that I need to try everything anyone suggests to me. Not wanting to do something you've never done before doesn't necessarily mean you're afraid."

"Like dating?" Philip asked.

"What?" Carina responded to his out-of-the-blue topic change. "What makes you think I'm afraid of dating?"

"It seems you don't date much. I mean real dates, not rich boy babysitting dates," Philip said. "Perhaps I'm wrong." Lightening the tension he added, "It's happened once or twice."

"Dating?"

"No," he said, smiling over his mug of cocoa, "being wrong."

Knowing him well enough despite their short acquaintance, she conceded her history—or part of it. In college she 'flew under the radar'—sometimes by choice, and sometimes unknowingly.

"Look at me," she said, tugging at her outfit. "Back then I dressed more thrift store than rich store, and still don't like name brands for the sake of name brands, honestly. Plus, I usually had my face in a book. I had male friends, but no serious boyfriend. I'm not the kind that attracts a lot of male attention, which I don't want anyway. College guys seemed to be more interested in the fashionistas and party girls."

Philip's lack of response to her longer than usual answer brought a frown to her eyes. "It wasn't a big deal, though, because I didn't have a lot of time for dating."

"Don't tell me," Philip said. "You were *busy.*"

"Ha, ha," she said. "I did keep busy with studies and friends. I didn't date a lot, but I wasn't a recluse." She paused as she remembered a specific instance. Philip noticed her hide a smile.

"I see that look, Carina," Philip said.

She laughed as she described one particular date, arranged by a mutual friend who was sure that her two friends would be a perfect match. Unfortunately, the matchmaker didn't know Carina as well as she thought.

"Elaborate please."

"The poor guy was looking for a Mary Bennett or a Charlotte Lucas," she said, describing the meekest of characters in a favorite classic novel.

"But discovered you were more like Lizzy Bennett?"

"Very good, Mr. Corelli," she smiled. "Are you an Austen connoisseur?"

"Connoisseur out of necessity," he said. "Mom and sister went through an Austen stage one summer. So you consider yourself an Elizabeth Bennett? I see you more as an Anne Elliott or Elinor Dashwood." His knowledge surprised Carina, but she turned back to their original topic, cutting short any further discussion.

"I don't like to ski," she said, not admitting it was the ski lift alone that she avoided. Her fear of heights had made her first experience on a lift terrifying. "I love the snow, though. Sledding the hills around my college campus—on trays snatched from the cafeteria—is one of my fondest memories."

"Sledding it is," Philip said. "We can get a few runs in tomorrow morning before lunch. I see you're on the list to help set it up at the chalet."

"But don't you want to ski?" Carina asked. "You shouldn't give up your slope time for me. I'll keep myself occupied."

"I'll have plenty of time," Philip said, "and I'm not going to take no for an answer, so don't bother arguing. I'm heading upstairs now. Good night, my dear."

In the morning while the others headed to the chair lift, Grayson carried the box of supplies in, and she sent him on his way to the slopes with a sincere thank you and a reminder to be safe. He had tugged her hat playfully as he promised to behave. She watched as he joined a group.

Of course, it was a group of females that eagerly greeted him.

Philip waited patiently and protectively. She ignored his scowl. "Grayson is harmless, so relax. I have to check in with the assistant chef so I know when to be here for lunch set up," she said.

"Fine," Philip pointed to the deck. "I'll meet you there in five minutes."

"You don't need to do this," Carina said. "I'll be fine. I'm going to wander the trails, take some pictures, watch you on the bunny slope…"

"Five minutes," he said. "Don't make me play the supervisor card."

Carina checked in with the hostess, apologizing for interrupting her during the busy breakfast time. The worker pointed out the chef that was helping with their lunch. The chef nodded. Carina smiled. Philip frowned. He had come back inside to retrieve Carina.

"Are you ready?" His curt tone caught her attention.

"Yes," she said. "What's wrong?"

Be careful, Philip. Emmie's voice was in his head. He forced a smile. "Nothing. Sorry, I was afraid you were going to back out."

"No way, mister," Carina said. "You talked me into this last night and now I'm looking forward to it."

They weren't the only adults on the sledding hill, a sizeable slope that needed a rope lift to reach the top. They made several runs and transferred to the alpine slide for one trip. They laughed the entire way down the winding track. Carina struggled to catch her breath as they both tumbled off the cart at the bottom.

"That was awesome!" Carina said. "I wish I had time to do that again." Philip felt the same, but more so for being able to be that close to her without raising questions.

Tess waved and called from the chair lift passing above them. "I got a great picture of you guys!" she said. "Looks like it was fun. I'll text it to you!"

As they walked back to the lodge, Carina shivered slightly, so Philip draped an arm loosely around her shoulders. Tess's text with their photo arrived as they reached the deck. They looked much happier than he and Britney ever had. When she grinned up at him, he tweaked her nose.

"Fun times, Miss Whitley. Thank you."

"You're welcome." She pulled off her gloves and patted his cheek. "As I reminded Grayson, I'll remind you. Behave. If you aren't careful someone may see you and misinterpret the attention you pay me. You don't want to be called a flirt and the group knows you're in a relationship." Her voice trailed off, before she added, "But I think it's good that Britney's not here." She pocketed her phone and waved him toward the ski rentals. "Go," she said. "Have fun."

As he walked away, he thought about her warning. Not sure he was willing to take her advice, he at least agreed with her sentiment about Britney. "I, too, think it's good that Britney's not here."

Inside the lodge, Carina paused to make sure Philip met up with their group, before seeking out the assistant chef who would be helping her. Chef Sebastian Arnez introduced himself. "Sorry I couldn't meet you this morning, but we were short-handed. Let me show you where you'll be setting up."

The buffet table was already set up, awaiting the lunch

spread, which she assumed would be sandwiches, soup, and salad. Carina found the box of supplies they'd brought from the chalet and placed a quiz sheet and pencil at each place. Although they weren't attending the retreat, as group leaders Emmie and Jay had asked everyone to fill out a form with interesting facts and background information on themselves. Emmie had created a master list of the answers. The quiz would reveal how much the class members learned about each other as they'd spent time together this morning and last night. Chef Arnez picked up one of the sheets and turned to Carina.

"So Miss Carina, I think your favorite author is Shakespeare, farthest you've been from home I'd say is Paris? You like classical music, and your favorite color is hmm...," he said, one eyebrow raised as he stared intensely, "blue."

Carina laughed. "I love Shakespeare, so I'll give you that point. Paris is a good guess, but London would be correct. Classical music is correct, and isn't blue the most popular favorite color?"

"True, but is it correct?" The handsome chef leaned closer.

"No," Carina said. "Mine changes almost daily, but that wouldn't surprise you if you knew that I work in an art museum. I did have an art professor whose favorite color was gray. It seemed strange until he taught us to see the subtle differences and wide variety of the under-appreciated color."

"Interesting," he said, "and understood. Food enthusiasts would be appalled to know that my favorite flavor of ice cream is vanilla." Her look held a hint of disbelief. He winked and whispered, "I'm not joking, but don't tell anyone. I'd lose my job."

"Ready, chef," the kitchen staff's call interrupted their levity. He and Carina arranged the trays of food. Technically these were sandwiches, but so much fancier than normal. The soup selections could've graced the menu of a five-star restaurant. Carina was an amateur cook, watched cooking shows whenever she had time, and sometimes tried her hand at a dish outside her normal fare. Her admiration grew exponentially when Sebastian brought out the desserts. The array looked like something out of a cooking magazine.

Working together they were done early, and he offered to show her some tricks of the trade.

"If I could make cheesecake this delicious, and decorate it like you have, I'd switch careers," she said. The kitchen staff was prepping for the lunch crowd, but Sebastian assured her they wouldn't be in the way.

"I worked the early breakfast shift, so I'm on break now. Normally I'd be on the slopes during my break, but this will be much more enjoyable," he said as he pulled out the remaining cheesecake ingredients. It was a quick recipe and once mixed, they talked while he set out the decorating supplies. Settling into such easy conversation, he ventured a question. "When I saw you earlier, was that your boyfriend?"

"Our relationship is complicated," she said, "and not always exactly what it appears to be." Knowing it was unlikely Chef Sebastian and Grayson would never cross paths, she explained their relationship in general terms. "I'm a safety net, basically. My boss described it as 'blue blood babysitting,' once. But honestly, it's not been too difficult."

"So, if I showed up in town one weekend," he said,

gaining confidence with her explanation, "you might consider going out with me? If you're not babysitting, that is."

Unused to such forthright attention, she blushed. She didn't date a lot, and never went out with men she didn't know well, but his interest was flattering. Not wanting to offend him, she used a tactic her roommates had perfected. Vagueness. "That sounds nice," she said. The oven buzzer sounded and while the small tarts cooled, Chef gave her some hints on decorating. He coached her through the first few decorations, then handed her a pastry bag. She was concentrating on the fancy flowers when she heard someone clear their throat. Thinking it was one of the staff, she continued to practice. The sound was repeated, louder this time.

"Carina," chef said. "I think your group has returned." He moved closer and lowered his voice. "I appreciate your enthusiasm, but your friend is trying to get your attention." She finally looked up.

"Philip! Oh, my," she said, wiping her hands on the towel Sebastian handed her. "Is everyone back already?" She fumbled with the apron ties in a rush to get back to her responsibilities. Sebastian moved her braid out of the way and untied it.

"Go on. We'll talk later," he said when she handed him the apron. He nodded to Philip whose return nod wasn't as cordial.

Grayson had saved her a seat, an encouraging move since it meant disappointment for a couple of the other ladies. Philip joined them which drew a trio of females who had won the open seat lottery. "Watch out," Carina elbowed Philip, "without Britney here you're now a target." The girls were her friends, and she knew their interest wasn't desperate.

As the meal wrapped up, Philip offered to make the quiz announcement. "Don't forget to fill these out before you head back out. We'll go over them tonight after dinner," he said. "You can give them to Carina, but I know where she put the answer sheet and will be accepting bribes."

"And you accused me of being the comic," she said as he sat down. The quizzes piled up beside her and she organized them to make the evening's reveal easier. Philip, Grayson, and several others volunteered to clear the tables. The kitchen staff would handle the buffet.

Philip dismissed the others as the work finished. He missed the return of the chef from his one trip down the slopes. Carina waved to Sebastian and he pointed to the kitchen and then his watch. She nodded, planning to meet him in a few minutes. She packed the quizzes back into the supply box as Philip rejoined her.

"So, what are we doing now?" Philip asked. "I've gotten my runs in, so I'm free to do whatever you'd like."

"Well, you're going to go enjoy yourself on the slopes," she said. "No way will I let you hold this over me years from now."

"I would never...." he said. She laughed as he clutched his chest. "C'mon, Carina. You can't just sit in here by the fire, sipping hot chocolate." When he saw her glance at the kitchen, he swallowed a growl. "A date with the chef? Really?"

"No, nosey," she said. "He's letting me know the tarts we made earlier are ready. On cue Sebastian held up the box of goodies. "I promise not to waste my afternoon relaxing by a cozy fire. I have plans." Those plans included exploring the resort's art gallery that featured local artists and talking to the children's program manager. Hopefully there would be time for a walk along one of the resort's trails taking photos for a children's art project.

"This is a *retreat*, Carina." Philip reminded her. "Do I need to define the word for you?" She started to push him toward the door when Sebastian interrupted their jousting to introduce himself. Philip pasted on a smile and greeted the chef cordially. The three of them talked for a few minutes before some of the novices called Philip to show them how to strap on their skis. "I'll be right back."

"So, he doesn't seem to be faking your relationship, Carina," the chef said, having observed her and Philip.

"Philip?" Carina confusion was short-lived. "Oh no, he's just a friend. My 'date' is Grayson." Pointing toward the cluster of females gathered around the young Mansfield on the deck, she clarified. "He's been well-behaved today, despite what you see right now," her voice trailed off as she realized that she didn't recognize any of the women. "There's still work to do, obviously. I need to rescue him."

Philip rejoined the chef as Carina headed away. The pair of men watched as she extricated Grayson from a group of women, none of whom were part of their group. The young man seemed relieved when she tugged him towards their dining area. He showed his appreciation by pulling her close and kissing her soundly on the cheek. "Great acting, ma'am," Philip said quietly as he watched her giggle at whatever nonsense he spouted.

"Acting?" Sebastian asked Philip, who had forgotten he had company.

"At least she better be acting," Philip said.

"We can always hope," Chef Arnez said. He smiled as

Carina released Grayson and turned to rejoin him and Philip. As she neared, he added, "Have a great afternoon on the slopes, Philip. I promise to take good care of Carina if she changes her mind and wants to join me in the kitchen. She'll be in good hands."

Philip glared at Sebastian but pasted on a grin when Carina headed his way. Her hug defrosted his gaze and replaced it with a hint of victory.

"Have fun, Philip," she said. "Be careful and behave."

He conceded the field with a simple, "You, too, Miss Whitley." He reached around her to grab his jacket that was conveniently hung on the nearest chair. He whispered, "Try to miss me a little bit."

Carina's attention on Philip's retreating form caused her to miss the knowing look from Sebastian. He would've loved to add his name to the list of men seeking her interest, but his hopes were waning. Still he invited her to join him in the kitchen, offering to show her the evening's menu. She declined.

"We'll be heading back to the chalet before dinner," she said, "which I'm sure will pale in comparison to what you'll be serving here. I have a meeting with the resort's activities director, and then I want to enjoy some of the trails I've heard so much about." He recommended the best trail for her and promised to call her the next time he was in her area. Two hours later, she was glad they had exchanged phone numbers.

Chapter 11
I hope you know I care

The alarm on the medical team's walkie talkies cut through the noise in the main dining room where another group enjoyed an early dinner. Chef Arnez was prepping the meat carving station when he saw the hostess pointing his way.

Someone was injured on the slopes. One of the medics waved Chef Arnez over, asking if he knew anyone from the group that was in the dining room earlier. "I have a phone number," he said. Before he could pull up Carina's number, one of the guys from the church burst into the lodge.

"Anyone know where Carina is? She's the girl that was setting up our lunch," the young man's word tumbled out as he tried to catch his. "Philip's been hurt and needs to go to the hospital."

"I'm on it," Sebastian said. "She's on the main trail. Let the kitchen staff know where I am."

"Take the backup ATV, Sebastian," the medic called to him. "We'll meet you back here. They're saying it's not serious, but a hospital visit is required."

Sebastian called Carina as he grabbed his jacket and the keys the medic had tossed to him. "Carina, it's Sebastian. Don't panic, but Philip's hurt. It's not serious, though. The medical staff is on their way to get him. Someone from your group came looking for you. Are you on the trail I recommended?"

"Yes," she said, "but I think I'm almost halfway around the loop."

"Head this way," Sebastian said, "I'm getting the ATV and coming to meet you. They told me to tell you it's not bad, but they'll have to send him to the hospital as a precaution."

There were few hikers on the trail so Sebastian reached Carina in a few minutes. She hopped onto the vehicle almost before he brought it to a stop. "Thanks, Sebastian," she said, catching her breath as he turned around and headed back down the trail. "You said he's not hurt badly? Will they take him to the hospital? Our group brought a car along with the bus, so do I need to get the keys? What happened? Are you sure he's okay? He probably did something crazy, like going on the black diamond slope. I'm going to put hi m in a time out if he did something foolish. He's going to be okay, though, right?"

"Yes, he's going to be fine. Hold on, I'm going to break some rules getting us back to the chalet as fast as I can."

Carina tightened her hold and Sebastian distracted her by asking if she'd gotten any good pictures on the trail. She didn't answer but nodded against his back. When they reached the lodge, the medical team hadn't arrived yet, so he continued to encourage her. He explained that Philip would likely be taken to the hospital in the resort's medical transport, which they used for non-emergency trips. Usually there were several trips every weekend.

While they waited, he warmed her up with hot chocolate. As the medical snowmobile came into view, they could see Philip sitting on the back, with his leg immobilized.

"He'd be on the stretcher if the injury was serious, Carina," Sebastian said. "He's going to be fine."

She nodded, finished her cocoa, and let him help her put her jacket back on. "Thank you, my friend. I'm glad you knew where I was," she said, adding with a smile, "and had my number."

"Of course," he replied. "No problem. I'm glad I was able to help." He handed her the camera she had been carrying on the trail, and he reached for her hand. She'd been gloveless when he found her, and wasn't surprised that it was still cold, so he warmed it between both of his. Despite the intimacy, she kept glancing at the snowmobile as it drew nearer. Sebastian knew he'd only have a few moments before they'd be interrupted.

"You and Philip," he said.

"Yes?" Carina's tone indicating her attention was still divided.

He placed her hat securely on her head and bent to meet her eyes. "You two need to be honest with each other," he said, "before it's too late." She had no chance to respond as the lead medic stepped into the dining hall and called for her.

Philip's sheepish grin greeted her when she reached his side. "I know, I know," he said. "I should've stayed on the bunny slope. That's what you're thinking."

"What happened?" Carina asked the group members

that had followed the medical team down the slopes. She ignored Philip.

"It wasn't his fault. It was…" One of the church members started to respond, but a quick glance from Philip stopped him abruptly.

"C'mon, Carina," Philip said, as the transport van arrived. "All this attention is embarrassing enough. Don't make me recount how dumb I was."

Sebastian brought to-go cups of hot chocolate for the group that had gathered. Although the medical staff told him that it was most likely a sprain, Philip's entire leg was splinted as a precaution. While they loaded him into the van, Carina sought out her new friend. She gave him a quick hug. As she turned around, she saw Philip's eyes narrow, so his comment as she climbed in the van didn't surprise her.

"You were awfully affectionate with a man you just met."

"I was thanking him. He found me on the trail and brought me back here to you."

"Oh," Philip said, then leaned around her to nod at the still watching chef. "He seems like a nice guy."

"He is," was Carina's simple response.

On the way to the hospital, Carina set aside her criticism and instead distracted Philip with a summary of her discussions with the resort's activities director. "They've been doing children and family activities at the lodge for years. The director is going to email me their program lists."

"Did you get a chance to check out the gift shop? I

heard they had an extensive artwork section. Is it mainly photography? Did you find anything interesting?"

"There was a wide variety of artwork and some interesting jewelry made by local artisans. I found a pair of earrings I liked, but they were out of my price range. I saw a few items I think Emmie would like, too, so I may have Jay look at the resort website. The clerk said the gift shop page is updated regularly." She kept up a running commentary, interspersed with the occasional, "Are you in a lot of pain? They said they didn't think it's broken."

Philip let her ramble on, content to have her close. He suspected she didn't realize she was holding his hand—perhaps to comfort him—or herself. Either way, his humor helped him ignore the pain and teasing her had become second nature. "When we get to the hospital, I know you'll be disappointed if they won't let you go back to the exam room with me."

She responded in kind. "I think you're confusing disappointment with relief."

"Ouch," Philip said. The medical attendant had ignored their conversation, but Philip's comment drew his attention.

"Are you in pain? We're pulling into the hospital now," the young woman said. "Are you hurting anywhere besides your ankle?"

"No, I'm good," Philip said, shooting a warning look at Carina who attempted to hide her laughter. At the triage desk, Philip paid her back.

"Your girlfriend can come into the exam room if you want," the triage nurse said as the medic wheeled him into the emergency room. Philip winked at Carina as she started to correct the mistake.

"Yes, please," he said. "She's not finished telling me how much of an idiot I was to get hurt." Once alone in the exam room, Carina punched his arm.

"Ow," he said.

"That didn't hurt," she said. "But if you call me Britney, you'll be dealing with more than a sprained ankle."

"If I had corrected her, you'd be pining away in the waiting room, worrying about me." He closed his eyes and settled back. "Can you rearrange the pillow for me, dearest?"

The doctor joined the couple, preventing her from 'rearranging' the pillow for him. "We're taking him next door for a quick x-ray. We'll be back in a minute. The nurse will bring in the paperwork for you to start filling out," he said. Philip handed her his wallet so she could access his insurance information. The movement jostled the leg and she bit her lip when he grimaced.

"I'll be okay, Carina," he said. "Don't miss me too much."

She sighed deeply. "I'll try."

As the technician wheeled him out of the room, he knew his life was heading for a crisis. He was slowly unfurling the white flag of surrender. His feelings for this lady, and even more so his growing attachment to her, were winning the battle.

It was only a sprain, but not a minor one. He'd be on crutches for at least a week and in a soft cast for three to four more. On the way back to the chalet, Philip dozed in the back seat with his leg propped up on their rolled-up jackets. The assistant pastor had sent one of the guys to the hospital with the minivan to retrieve them. When he stirred as they arrived, Carina asked if he wanted her to call Britney to let her know what happened. "No," he said, not opening his eyes. The pain meds were making him sleepy. "She's having a blast in Aspen if her social media posts are any indication. No use in bothering her."

The group gave him a hero's welcome, thanking him for adding some excitement to the weekend. When Grayson approached Carina, Philip interrupted. "Hey, Grayson, can you move that stool over a bit? I need to prop this monstrosity up. Carina's going to tattle to the doctor if I don't follow the rules to the letter." When the younger man complied, Philip warned him. "Don't tell her what happened. It was an accident. You didn't mean for me to get hurt."

"I know, Philip, but I was an idiot. I shouldn't have been grandstanding like I was," he said.

"The fact that you're acknowledging your mistake shows your intentions," Philip said. "No need to bring Carina into it." He hoped Grayson would agree despite the confused look in his face.

Their delay at the hospital meant that dinner was nearly ready when they arrived. "Way to get out of dinner duty, Corelli," one of the guys called. "You're a lazy bum."

"You got me!" Philip said. "I thought I had everyone fooled. Now you just have to convince Miss Whitley and Grayson to feel sorry enough for me to come keep me company."

Carina relented and let the rest of the group serve her. Philip sensed her discomfort, but didn't give in. He knew she needed to learn to accept help instead of always being the one serving. "Relax, my dear," he said. "You have two handsome men giving you their undivided attention. Enjoy it."

Their normal banter peeked out again. "Two? Grayson's here. Who else?"

"Ha, ha, ha," Philip said. "I'm mortally wounded and you're teasing me. I'm crushed."

Grayson watched the interplay with a slightly confused look. His 'relationship' with Carina was superficial, as agreed, but the comfortable companionship between Carina and Philip seemed foreign to him. Carina saw his confusion.

"So, Grayson, did you enjoy your day?" she asked as she accepted the plate of food one of the girls handed her. She missed the look between the men flanking her.

"Yes," he said. "It was interesting."

After dinner, the group had a time of sharing. The majority of the tales were funny stories from the day. No one mentioned Philip's crash. Slowly, the assistant pastor who was leading the retreat this weekend, turned the conversation to spiritual matters.

"We'd like to hear your faith stories," he said. "This is optional. No pressure for everyone, or anyone, to share, but we've found that voicing how our Heavenly Father has moved in your life is always encouraging to others."

Several of the group shared immediately. Some had grown up in a church-going family and come to take ownership in their spiritual journey early in life. One of the men shared about his dysfunctional family and his dark journey through addiction. His college roommates were the ones that invited him to a church retreat like this one and it had turned his life around.

Grayson spoke up soon after. "I'm not sure about this God or faith stuff yet," he admitted. "But you guys have been super chill with me. I know I've used some language that I shouldn't have. Sorry," he said. Looking around the room he saw smiles and nods of compassion. "I still have questions, but this weekend has been totally different than anything I've ever experienced."

Philp heard Carina's soft sigh. Knowing eyes were focused their direction, he squeezed her hand under the counter, without making eye contact.

After a long pause, Philip decided to share his story. "My faith journey could be described as a series of detours. I grew up in a large family. Most of you know that Emilia Lazlo is my aunt." When he saw the questions on some faces, he explained the age range of his mom's siblings. "Although I only have one brother and one sister, both younger than me, my aunts, uncles, and numerous cousins are all close. When I was young, going to church was a given, but later I chose a different, and quite bumpy path." He briefly explained the influence of peers in high school and college, and without details about Britney, the recent turn around that God had orchestrated. "I'm thankful for the faith of my relatives, but I know not everyone is born into a loving, believing family. Sometimes they may feel that a path away from God is inevitable, but I know God can break those chains.

117

Bad decisions that you make or that others make, don't have to define our own faith story."

"Well said, Philip," the pastor said. "I think that's a great place to end. Remember, God can heal all hurts. He doesn't always remove the scars, but he can ease the pain."

Philip reached for Carina's hand, but she pulled away, shaking her head slightly. Pieces of her story that he'd glimpsed over the past weeks were starting to fall into place.

"I smell brownies!" One of the men yelled after the pastor's prayer. Grayson moved to help rearrange the chairs. Carina started to get up to help but Philip swung her bar stool around to face him.

"Your childhood was very different than mine," he said. It was a statement not a question. "I won't ever pressure you to share your story, but I hope you know I care." There was only silence from Carina but he saw the tears gathering. "You have someone to talk to, though, don't you?"

"Yes, I do." She nodded and blinked away the tears. "And yes, I talk to her regularly."

Breakfast prep started early the next morning. The bus would be leaving by nine to make sure the group returned to the church by mid-afternoon.

Philip had slept on the couch so he didn't have to navigate the stairs. The ground floor had a full bath, so he had showered carefully, using the waterproof cover for his cast that the doctor had provided.

He was struggling with his suitcase and crutches when

Carina arrived downstairs. "Need some help, sir?" she asked. Philip tugged his unbuttoned shirt closed, dropping one of his crutches in the process. "Looks like you need help dressing, at least." He couldn't chance her offering to button his shirt, so he waved the remaining crutch toward his luggage.

"That monster tried to kill me," he said. "Can make sure it's safely stowed in the pile by the door?" While she wheeled the carry-on sized suitcase away, Philip fumbled with the buttons on his shirt. It took two attempts to button it correctly. *Why is it so hot in here?*

The pastor was on the list for helping this morning and had already begun to crack eggs into a pitcher. His wife stirred the orange juice concentrate in a separate pitcher. Philip hobbled over and prepped the large frying pan for the eggs. The ladies got the biscuits into the oven, and heated the pre-cooked bacon in the microwave.

Philip patiently stirred the eggs in the large skillet. Several minutes later, he called Carina over. "Something's wrong with this stove. These eggs aren't cooking at all."

Carina glanced at the orange mixture now swirling and boiling in the pan. She got a whiff as Philip stirred. She tried to choke back a laugh, but was unsuccessful. "Oh, Philip." An inability to talk meant she merely waved toward the pitcher on the counter behind him.

He looked from the pan to the pitcher. Same color, same texture…or almost the same. "Oh, no. This is orange juice." Alarmed at what sounded like screams from the kitchen, the pastor and wife hurried to the outburst before realizing Philip and Carina were laughing. Seeing that the pair would be unable to continue, the pastor grabbed Grayson, who had finally appeared downstairs, and they dumped out the now-warm orange juice and prepped another pan for the eggs. The lack of juice at breakfast became a running joke with the group for years.

Chapter 12
I'm more than okay

The retreat had been eye-opening for Philip. He'd suspected Britney had been texting Grayson during the retreat, but the young man's answers to his leading questions implied that Carina's faux boyfriend was not interested in the alluring Britney. When she suggested another weekend visit, Philip cringed when she giggled, "Carina won't mind, I'm sure."

Even though the pace of work for the opening of the museum no longer occupied every moment of Carina's day, Philip made it clear that Britney would have to entertain herself during work hours on Friday. A familiar pout accompanied her acquiescence so he assured her of his plans for a quiet dinner out and a movie. He'd made those plans so she'd be out of Carina's way for most of the day. He sent a text telling Carina to treat herself to a relaxing afternoon and evening.

Boss's orders

You can't tell me what to do. You're not the boss of me.

Technically, no, but, really, Carina. Go to a spa, go shopping, do whatever it is you girls do to relax. We won't be back until close to midnight.

The evening with Britney strained his patience. A renewed push for him to 'live up to the Corelli name,' annoyed him. Her mention of Grayson, and how he didn't hide his wealth or status, brought more suspicion. He suspected she had been texting Grayson during the retreat, but the young man's answers to his leading questions implied that Carina's faux boyfriend was not interested in the alluring Britney.

The movie did nothing to lighten his mood but Britney seemed oblivious. As they arrived at the apartment building, he dreaded disturbing Carina's evening.

"Carina may be asleep, so we need to be as quiet as possible," he said.

"I can think of something quiet we can do," Britney smiled as she wound her arms around his neck. He resisted Britney's goodnight advances, shushing her and guiding her through the apartment door. "Good night, Britney."

He waited until she closed the bedroom door before checking on Carina. The smell of freshly baked brownies and the shopping bag from a well-known day spa encouraged him.

Good for you, he thought.

When he saw her stir, he paused to see if she would wake up, but when she settled back to sleep, he carefully tucked the blanket over her uncovered feet. Leaning over slightly, he whispered, *Goodnight, my dear.*

Deciding to try one more time to clarify his relationship with Britney, while battling his deepening connection with Carina, Philip proposed an impromptu dinner party the next night. Inviting Tess, Lincoln, Grayson, and Carina to join him and Britney seemed the easiest way to evade her attempts to be alone with him.

Philip planned a traditional Greek meal. Carina offered to help. Jay and Emilia had treated her to several delicious meals, Greek from Emilia's family, Italian from Jay's, and the unique fusion that the couple had developed. "I loved the Greek food and I'd love to learn how to make some of those dishes," she said when he described the menu. His plan included stuffed grape leaves, called dolmades, baklava that Emilia made and dropped off earlier, and tzatziki with grilled chicken and pita chips.

Britney spent the day shopping while Philip worked. She hadn't made it back to Carina's apartment, where she was again staying overnight, before Carina headed to Philip's to help with dinner. Tess and Lincoln arrived, set the table, and were now admiring Philip's antique and first edition copies of classic literature.

Having prepared more filling for the dolmades than he needed, Philp ran out of serving pans. Carina was in the middle of rolling the grape leaves around the rice mixture, so he headed to her apartment to get another platter and some lemons for the tzatziki dip.

"I'll be back tomorrow," he joked as he grabbed his crutches. Her apartment was on the other end of the building and although he'd been gaining speed with the crutches, he sometimes hopped along when Carina wasn't looking. 'Doctor' Carina was incredibly strict. Not only did she play the role of chauffer, but she also became the enforcer, insisting that he follow the actual doctor's orders. 'No weight on the booted foot for two weeks.'

He started to knock on Carina's door to give Britney a warning that someone was entering. A man's voice reached him. When he unlocked the door with the spare key Carina had given him, Philp was greeted by his fiancée-in-name-only, wrapped in a bath towel, moving slowly toward a terrified Grayson Mansfield.

"You wouldn't dare," Grayson said, his voice rising in alarm. In his haste to back away from the advancing predator, he knocked over a pile of art history books on the coffee table. The noise from the books, and Britney's focus on her prey, meant she missed her fiancé's entrance. Her inattention was obvious.

"Try me," Britney smiled. "What makes you think I haven't done it before?"

"Well, what do we have here?" Philip said as he maneuvered his crutches through the door. "Looks slightly familiar to me."

Grayson's words tumbled out. "Britney said she needed help taking something down the hall for you guys. I just got here. I would never, ever,..."

Philip's raised hand silenced the younger man. "Wait for me in the hall." Grayson obeyed.

"Miss Frost, it seems our relationship has come to an end. I'll send you a text in a few minutes with a suggested wording for the dissolution of our so-called engagement." When she started to protest, his simple glare stopped her. "Don't even try, Britney. I no longer care for my reputation that you threatened to tarnish. You can make this as painful or as easy as you choose. Blame the breakup on me, but I wouldn't recommend that. When the truth comes out, and it eventually will if you continue with this behavior, *your* reputation will be the one that suffers."

A defiant chin didn't hide her angry blush. He no longer cared. Grabbing the pans, lemons, and the spare keys that were on the kitchen counter, he made his way past Britney, careful to stay out of her reach. At the doorway he turned. "You have ten minutes to vacate Carina's apartment. I'll call you a cab. It will be downstairs in fifteen minutes. You can keep the engagement ring—it holds no sentimental value to me. I would only auction it off for charity, but you can do with it what you will. Goodbye, ma'am. I hope you find what you *need*," he said, "and for your own good, I hope it's not what you *want*."

Grayson paced in the hallway. "This is the plan, son," Philip said as he handed him the serving platter and lemon when they reached the door of his apartment. "Britney's decided to go home early, and I found you in the hallway. We'll leave it at that until you get a chance to explain everything to Carina. Tell her I'll be just a minute." He pulled out his phone to compose the text to Britney. "Go on in. Relax and try to enjoy the evening." Philip waited for the door to close, then texted Britney:

As promised, I'm sending a suggested announcement for your social media platforms. I will post something similar, making it clear that you were the one that is ending the relationship. Should you do anything to imply otherwise, or to implicate anyone else, I will answer those statements with the truth. I truly do wish you the best, Britney. Here's what you should post:

It is with heavy heart that I announce I have ended my engagement to Philip Corelli. We are parting amicably and wish each other the best.

Philip nodded at Carina as he limped to the kitchen. "It's all good," was his only comment. She let the obvious ruse set the tone for the evening.

As he filled the water glasses a few minutes later, he heard the cab arrive. He moved to the window and pulled the curtains back. Britney saw the movement, glanced at the window, and blew him a kiss, then laughed. Philip was relieved that he didn't have to do more to get her out of Carina's apartment.

As hoped, the meal and post-dinner board game helped Grayson recover. Philip suggested that he offer to help Carina in the kitchen as Tess and Lincoln were leaving. It didn't take long for the confessions to begin. "Carina, I have a couple things to explain," Grayson said as he dried dishes. "First, I'm sure Philip's kept this quiet, and he told me not to tell you, but I have to. I was the reason he got hurt on the slopes. A girl, not from our group, challenged me to a race. I was stupid. I'm sorry I didn't tell you before."

"I figured there was more to the story than what Philip told me," Carina said. "I'm sure you didn't mean for him to get hurt." She handed him a pan to dry. "You said 'first.' Was there something else?"

He summarized the scene in her apartment. His admission encouraged Carina. "I did enjoy the flirting at first," he said, "but I told her my family said, 'no way.' That seemed to make her come on stronger. She kept texting me during the retreat. I told her I wasn't interested and finally blocked her. After the retreat, I told her again I wasn't interested. I'm pretty sure their engagement is done," he said.

While they were talking, Philip busied himself with cleaning up the board game and dessert dishes. As he stopped outside the kitchen's swinging doors, he heard Carina's concern.

"Is Philip okay?" she asked.

"Definitely," Grayson assured her.

Philip, still out of sight, smiled. *I'm more than okay....now...*

Grayson returned home the next week. Carina received a large bouquet of flowers thanking her for the changes his parents saw in him. She learned on Sunday that they had also sent thanks to the church leaders. The welcome and grace shown to Grayson at the retreat were life-changing for their son.

Three weeks of carpooling had gone smoothly. At the first follow-up appointment the doctor added another week of crutches. The argument over continuing the carpooling didn't last long. Close friends recognized Carina's protectiveness, but Philip experienced it firsthand.

"What part of 'this is not a democracy' did you not understand?" She posed as she held the elevator door for him.

"You're a tyrant," he said.

"You're welcome," she responded. "Now stop complaining and tell me how the meeting with the board went last night. Any earth-shattering news?"

Philip laughed, knowing how she would react to the first issue on the docket. Grayson's family was thrilled with their son's turnaround. "We had to talk them out of making a huge donation in your name," Philip said, clutching the dashboard as Carina pumped the brakes. "Whoa, there, ma'am. Remember I'm still recovering from a major injury."

"Sorry," she said. "What are you saying? Please tell me they didn't do anything outrageous."

"I'm sworn to secrecy." He held up a hand. "I can tell you that they settled on something a bit more subtle."

"Let's hope so," Carina said. She discovered later that their appreciation took the form of a scholarship for underprivileged students to attend specialized art camps. "Tell me about the rest of the meeting."

Philip filled her in. Most of the meeting centered around the final plans for the building, funding issues, and the ongoing hiring progress. Carina listened patiently but was more interested in the discussion of the children's programs. Philip had good news, but knew the Mr. Manchester wanted to share it with her.

"It went well," he said, gauging his words carefully. They were stopped at a long light, so he had her full attention. "Not everything is finalized, so I don't want you to get your hopes up too high." He saw her shoulders slump, so he took her hand. "Trust me?"

She nodded. The small signs of affection Philip showed over the last two weeks seemed natural and Carina had begun to respond in kind. Philip had sensed a history behind her tensing when they danced at the first fundraiser, but she had relaxed so quickly he was hopeful. He wanted her to trust him and to feel safe. At the least sign of discomfort, he always backed off. Their camaraderie at the retreat, the closeness of the sled ride, and now his literal reliance on her help walking, encouraged him. He did not take for granted that she wasn't afraid of him or leery of his closeness. Protecting her became purposeful.

"Let's talk about something else," he suggested. During the last two weeks, their morning conversations had ranged from opinions about politics, sports teams, television and movies, and a heated discussion of the rise of technology in kindergarten. Philip longed for information about Carina but he knew walls would go up if he pushed too hard. Today he took a chance. "Where do you go every night?" Bluntness worked.

"Are you on the night patrol now, Philip?" She raised an eyebrow, not taking her eyes off the crowded morning traffic. "Which night in particular has you curious?"

"All of them," he said. "I know you go to the gym a couple times a week." When she slowed the card, he added, "Don't freak out. I only know that because I saw it on your calendar when we were discussing your taxi service and determining when my hours didn't correspond with yours. I know you like to have a full schedule, but it seems to me you don't have a lot of 'down' time. Emmie mentioned tutoring and volunteering."

"Well, Mr. Nosey, in no particular order I tutor at the church's evening homework help center, I go to the college library to research ideas for the children's program, and yes, I go to the gym a couple times a week…for dance class."

"Ballet?"

"Yes," she said, "as you are aware from our house-hunting expedition. I've been dancing since I was young."

Philip wanted to pursue the 'since I was young' statement, but stopped himself. Picking what he thought was a safe segue, he mentioned the local ballet company's upcoming production of Cinderella. "Have you gone to any of their shows?" When silence met his question, he grew suspicious. As they pulled into the office parking lot, he pressed her. "You're in it, aren't you?"

"Way to go, Sherlock," she said. "I'm proud of you." She gathered her purse and satchel of research that she studied during her lunch hour, and came around the car to get his crutches. "This afternoon, I get to grill you on your extra-curricular activities."

Despite the pace predicated by the crutches, Philip made it to his office twenty minutes early—time enough to check out the ballet company's website. Since the one-night show was less than a month away, programs would be finalized and he could confirm her participation. He clicked on the cast tab. Starring as the Cinderella's Fairy Godmother was Carina Whitley. He made a quick call to Emmie as he pulled out his wallet and purchased the four closest seats withing minutes. He didn't plan to tell Carina and swore Emmie to secrecy. It took all his self-control to keep it to himself on the way home.

Chapter 13
It's been fun

With the opening of the museum looming less than three months away, Philip's days filled with checking acquisitions as they arrived and supervising the warehouse renovations. The call for submissions from the community started next week so plans for displaying the chosen pieces, along with winners from the campus submissions, needed to be made. Carina ordered the framing supplies for the community and college pieces as well as for the Mansfield collection pieces that would need to be repaired or reframed.

Many of the afternoon rides home involved recapping their days. Philip spent most of his time at the warehouse, in his new office. Mr. Mansfield's office, and therefore Carina's, would remain in their temporary space at the college until after the grand opening. Philp missed seeing her during the day and relished these commutes and conversations. Their ride would be longer today as they planned a stop for groceries.

"First, sir," Carina said one afternoon as Philip hobbled to the car.. "I'm upset with you for not telling me the news."

Feigning ignorance, Philip raised his brows. "News?"

"Nice try," Carina said. "Don't quit your day job to become an actor." She held the door open while he shoved the crutches in the trunk of her car. "Mr.

Mansfield told me the children's program was approved."

"Congratulations," he smiled. "I took an oath not to tell you. You wouldn't want me to lose my job, would you? You'd miss me too badly."

"Badly," she repeated. "Not the word I would've used, but we'll go with that." After his laughter subsided, she changed topics. "Did the last delivery of the Mansfield's art contain any surprises?" Carina asked. "They were eclectic collectors, weren't they?" She had seen the last batch which contained mainly contemporary pieces, but knew that the first had been primarily early American art. The most prized pieces would be the last to arrive. Heavily insured, a special courier would deliver them a few days before the opening.

She and Philip discussed the more unusual pieces, including an odd set of sculptures that had caused a stir. These came from a recent exhibit at another museum and their curator sent the catalog from the exhibition to Philip before the shipment. Unfortunately, the entry for the trio of pieces contained no dimensions, history, or descriptive information. Philip spent several days and numerous phone calls trying to determine their origin and artist. Mr. Mansfield was little help. "I remember those," he had said. "Atrocious, I thought, but apparently highly sought after. My great uncle had eccentric taste."

"I've placed a call to Grayson's father," Philip said. "I'm hoping he can help. I can't determine where, or if, to display them if I don't know how large they are." He had shown Carina the photos form the catalog. "What did you think?" he asked.

"I like them," she said. "They're reminiscent of trees in a forest or people on a journey. I know that sounds like two different interpretations, but they give me the sense of movement. They're organic, natural." When he shook his head, she paused. "You don't like them?"

"No, that's not it," he said. "You're incredible, that's all. I can't imagine doing this without you."

"Doing what?"

After a longer pause, he answered. "This museum stuff," he mumbled. '*Life*,' was what he wanted to say. Thankfully, she was now concentrating on the traffic, wary of another driver who seemed to be in a hurry.

"It's been fun," she said. "I'm glad it's with you."

"With me?" Philip held his breath. "What do you mean?"

"You're unusual. Not all curators believe that someone without their credentials can have a valid opinion about art." As they pulled into the grocery store parking lot, she turned to him. "Have I ever thanked you for that?"

"No thanks needed," he said. Carina had offered to do his shopping for him, but he declined. "Let's see if they're giving out samples today. I'm starving."

"What do you think you're doing?" When he left his crutches in the car, she blocked his way, arms on her hips.

"Practicing," he said. "Today's my last day with crutches, so I'm only cheating by a few hours." When she didn't move, he leaned in, almost nose to nose. "It's gotta be tomorrow somewhere." Watching her expression change from chagrin to exasperation to humor, was fascinating. The self-control needed to resist kissing her was excruciating.

"Okay, young man," she finally said. "If you don't behave, though, I won't let you get a cookie."

The shopping event was entertaining. Philip

befriended a family in the produce section and quizzed their youngest, a boy of about two years old, on his colors. When Carina joined him, he introduced her to the mom. "This is Carina Whitley," he said. "She's working on a children's art program for the new museum. We should have information out about it in the next couple of weeks. Feel free to call us with any questions." He took out a business card, begged a pen from Carina, and wrote her name on the back. "It's gonna be fun!" he said to the kids as he handed the card to the oldest.

In the frozen food section, Philip grabbed a couple pizzas. "Can I treat you to dinner? Not gourmet, but filling."

"You should contact the company and suggest that for their new ad campaign," she said as she put them on his side of the basket. "I have plans tonight, though."

"Of course," he said, planning to make this his line of questioning in the car. Traffic had worsened so they had a longer ride to the apartment, offering an ideal time for him to fill in the blanks of his Carina information.

"Plans tonight?" he asked. "What could possibly be better than a delicious meal with me?" He laughed when she tapped her chin and started her list.

"Laundry, minor surgery, changing a tire in a rainstorm…shall I go on?"

"Ouch," he clutched his chest.

"Normally I'd be at the animal shelter tonight," she said. "They have extended hours a couple times a month, but with the show so close, I have ballet rehearsal tonight."

"Do you ever take a night off? I see you coming in awfully late sometimes, too. You're staying safe, aren't' you?"

"Yes, I do, and yes, I am," she said. "Thank you for your concern." Her tone had lost its playfulness, so he dropped the topic. She helped him get his groceries in, frowning as he carried his crutches. He insisted on helping her with her bags, since her apartment was the furthest from the elevator. At her door, he took her hand, emboldened when she didn't pull away. "I'm sorry if I overstepped," he said. "I can't help it. I do care about you, Carina." He kissed her hand. "Is that okay?" Knowing his question could be taken several ways, he smiled when she replied simply…and didn't pull her hand away.

"Yes. Thank you, Philip. I'll see you bright and early tomorrow."

When Emilia called later that night to check on Philip's healing progress, he mentioned the progress he'd made with Carina. After the end of his 'engagement' to Britney, he'd admitted what the Lazlos already knew. He was falling fast for Carina.

"She's hiding something," he said. "I have a feeling it's painful and that's part of the reason she stays busy."

"And also why she's everyone's protector," Jay said. "I've noticed that since we met her months ago. It will be hard for her to let someone protect her in return. It would be a huge step of vulnerability."

Emmie and Jay promised to pray for the right timing for sharing, if that was what was best for Carina. Even if she never opened up, they wanted her to know they genuinely cared and loved her.

Deciding on a new plan of action, Philip surprised Carina the next morning. "So, I've spent so much time being nosy about you, I'm going to give you a chance to ask me anything. I'd even be willing to share embarrassing childhood stories, although I'm sure Emilia, my parents, and my siblings would correct my recollections and most likely have many more to add."

Carina knew he had a younger sister Cassandra in college and a younger brother, Gino, in his second year of law school. Philip's mom was the oldest of four children, and she and his dad lived in Florida but traveled often to visit family. Carina's first question allowed Philip to fill in the gaps. "Dad is a software engineer, owns his own small company, so they have as much free time as they want. Mom is the artist in the family," he said. "You've seen her work. Most of the watercolors at Emmie's place are hers." He spent the rest of the morning's ride listing the other aunts, uncles, and cousins. It was an extensive inventory. As they pulled into his reserved parking space, he donned his best strict teacher voice. "Are you ready for your quiz?" When she laughed, he added, "Young lady, this is not funny. Did you not realize that you'd be accountable for the information you've been given? For shame."

"I'm pleading inaccurate information given by the instructor. Nowhere on the syllabus does it list this chapter," she said. "I'll report you to the head of the department if you dock my grade. How cruel to dump so much information and not allow me to even take notes. Your 'rate my professor' scores are going to plummet."

He laughed, but took the opportunity to test the waters. "Well, I hope your family story is as riveting as mine." He saw the emotional wall immediately rise. *Well, that was a mistake.*

"I'll be framing all day and working the gift shop at lunch," Carina said as they pulled into the warehouse parking lot. The timing worked against Philip, giving her a reason to ignore his prying. "You did say Emilia could take you home today, right? I think I'll be here late and need to be at rehearsal again tonight."

Philip simply nodded. *Good job, buddy. One step forward, three steps back.*

That afternoon Carina sat across from Mira once again. "Twice in a few weeks, Carina," Mira said, "but I don't sense alarm. What prompted this appointment? Anything to do with the gentleman you mentioned before?"

"The retreat happened," Carina said, "and then his engagement ended." She described the events, along with the laughter, that forced her and Philip closer. "Riding together for weeks, working together on a major project, and living in the same building means I'm with him all the time."

"By choice or by chance?" Mira asked.

"Yes." Carina laughed. "Both? I imagine having a brother might be like this. I feel safe with him, but a little more nervous since his engagement is over."

"Nervous? Why do you think that is?" Mira asked. "You say you feel safe, but has he done anything to make you uncomfortable?" She paused and she saw Carina's attention waver. "You're blushing, my dear."

"I feel like the silly girls in romantic novels," Carina said. "I've always thought they were silly, riding through life on their emotions."

"I sense a 'but.' You're attracted to him, and that confuses you?" Mira asked. "Or does it comfort you?"

"It surprises me, I think," Carina said. She fell silent as she thought about why she'd called Mira for an appointment. "There's a problem, though." The 'interrogation,' as she called the conversation during the last car ride, frightened her. "I know I've acted differently since then, and I'm sure it won't take long for him to call me on it."

Mira's advice encouraged her. "Trust your faith, be ready to share as much or as little as you want. You trust him, I can tell. Don't be afraid to be more than friends."

Carina left, ready to be vulnerable with Philip, but with fear lingering at the edge of her mind.

Chapter 14
I'll let you figure it out

A new Asian fusion restaurant opened a few blocks from campus. Philip suggested they get out of the office. "We both need a break," he said. "I know we have to get the publicity campaign finalized, but my head's spinning."

The arrival of their order of Asian pulled pork tacos and roasted cauliflower paused their discussion of Mr. Mansfield's preferences for the social media ads. Or rather, the discussion of how to convince him of the need for social media ads. Silence reigned as the delicious, messy meal took their undivided attention.

Philip paused long enough to take a drink to cool off the spiciness. Carina reached across the table and wiped the sauce off his chin. "I was saving that for later," he said.

"Sure you were," she said. "This is delicious, but I'm stuffed. I'm going to ask for a to-go box unless you want to finish the rest."

He shook his head but stuffed in another forkful.

"Miss Ree! Miss Ree!" A child's voice saved Philip from Carina's scolding. A young girl pulled her mother toward their table. "Mommy! It's my teacher, Miss Ree!"

Carina scooted her chair back in time to accept the enthusiastic hug from the youngster. "Hello Mei! How are you?" She introduced Mei and her mother to Philip, explaining the Mei was one of her ballet students. As typical of children, seeing an adult outside of their usual environment was exciting.

"What are you doing here? This is my mommy's work. Are you working here now? Is this your boyfriend?" The child launched her questions with lightning speed. Her mom intervened.

"Let's leave Miss Ree to her lunch, Mei," her mom said. "So sorry, Miss Whitley."

"No problem," Carina said. "This is our first time here and the food is delicious." She turned to Mei. "I'm going to go refill my drink, do you want to help me?"

"We're almost ready to leave, but please join us so you'll have a seat," Philip said, offering a seat to Mei's mother. She thanked him and clarified her daughter's description of her employment.

"My husband and I own the restaurant, so I'm glad you enjoyed it," she explained. "Sorry about my daughter's barrage of questions. Carina has done a magnificent job with the little ones at the dance studio. She has the patience of a saint. As you witnessed, Mei is a bit much sometimes, and I know there are others just as challenging in the class." On cue, Mei returned, without Carina who was grabbing the take-out box.

"Mr. Philip, Miss Ree says you work for her," Mei said, then repeated her most important question. "Are you her boyfriend?"

"We work together, Miss Mei," Philip said, then bent

down to whisper the rest of his response. "And no, I'm not her boyfriend…yet." Seeing the little girl's face light up, he winked. "Don't tell her, though. I want to surprise her someday soon." He distracted her with questions about her ballet class and her favorite food at the restaurant. When Carina returned, they said their goodbyes and both received big hugs from Mei.

"You're amazing," Philip said stopping beneath a shade tree as they walked back to campus. "According to Mei's mom you've turned a room full of kindergartners into talented ballerinas."

"It's one of the highlights of my week," Carina said. "I began dancing when I was a bit older than Mei, but it changed my life."

Philip heard the change in her voice, but didn't press for an explanation. He'd chosen to be patient, sensing knowing she was hiding a sadder history. Still, his growing attraction was difficult to hide. His thoughts ran through his mind in moments, but the silence was long enough to elicit Carina's notice.

"What's wrong, Philip? Why are you staring at me like that?"

In his head he answered. *"I want to kiss you,"* but wisely he verbalized a safer response. "Why?" he asked. "Why do you think, Carina?"

"I have no idea," she said.

"Honestly, Miss Whitley?" He leaned closer and tucked her hair behind her ear. "You have no idea what I'm thinking right now?" He watched her eyes widen. The sounds of the traffic behind him shook him back to reality. He grinned and slipped his arm around her shoulders as they continued their walk. "I'll let you figure it out. Hopefully sooner rather than later."

"Emilia, dearest aunt, I have an urgent question," Philip called her a few days later. "After my gaffe earlier this week, and despite the progress I've made since then, I now am faced with a conundrum."

"Sounds ominous," Emmie said, "Either that or you've stumbled upon a vocabulary list from middle school."

"You're amusing," he said. Tess and Lincoln's wedding was Saturday night. Philip wanted to ask Carina to be his date, but now was unsure. "I feel like a middle school boy, honestly. She's not ignoring me, so I think she's forgiven me for asking about her family. Should I risk it?"

"Yes!" Emmie said. "A wedding among co-workers is a perfect place to make a first appearance as a couple, even if you only offer to ride together. You've been cast-free for a week and haven't had any repercussions. Say you want to pay her back for all the chauffeuring she did. Maybe phrasing it like that, and not as a date, will be more palatable."

"Because going on a date with me would be so distasteful?"

"Your words, not mine, nephew dear," she laughed. "No, I mean no matter what you two do from now on, your interest in her is apparent to *everyone*…except maybe Carina. The fact that she doesn't avoid you looks like she's interested, too." Knowing that Carina might ask the Lazlos for a ride, the aunt and nephew schemed.

Emilia would work in Jay's odd firehouse schedule as a reason for not being able to commit to even attending the wedding. "It's only a small stretch of the truth, and I'll only use it if she asks me."

Heaven smiled on Philip the next morning as the elevator opened to Carina, her arms full of boxes. He grabbed the ones slipping and held the elevator door with his foot. "Playing Santa today, are we Miss Whitley?"

"I wish," she said. "Christmas is my favorite holiday."

Philip added the tidbit to his Carina list. Using the opening, he delivered his question. "How do you feel about weddings?" The lump in his throat brought back memories of the middle school years he'd discussed with Emilia.

"Good food, dancing, a chance to dress up," she said. "What's not to like?"

"I agree," he said. "What time do you want me to pick you up for Tess and Lincoln's wedding on Friday? I owe you lots of commuting hours, you know." He watched the blue eyes visible above her stack of boxes. Concern grew when her brows furrowed. He swallowed surprise when she answered.

"The wedding is at five-thirty, across town," she said. "How does four-thirty sound?"

"Perfect," he said. "Where do you want these?" The boxes gave him a chance to recover. He texted Emilia before he reached his office. She responded with a happy face, praying hands, and a dancing dog.

Both Tess's mom and Mrs. Stafford were avid thrift store shoppers. Neither family was wealthy by anyone's standards, but the scene as Philip and Carina entered the rustic barn-turned-wedding-venue was spectacular. Strings of twinkling lights and pots of azaleas strategically placed around the hall made it clear that elegance always didn't demand extravagance.

Carina's tea length light blue dress swirled around her as they hurried up the stairs. Tess had texted in panic, asking Carina to come to the bride's changing room. "I'll be right back," Carina told Philip. "Find us a seat." He watched her disappear behind the stage, and could finally breathe again. When she'd met him in the lobby less than an hour ago, he'd forgotten how. Her hair was pinned to one side, the long curls over one shoulder. The strapless dress set off the long aquamarine earrings and necklace. Philip blinked again at the memory. *She has no idea how beautiful she is.*

She was back in a few minutes and slipped into the chair next to him. "Minor hair pin emergency. Disaster averted." She held up her wrist, now bare. "Also, she needed something borrowed and blue. My bracelet provided both."

"You look lovely," he said, "with or without your bracelet."

She squeezed his arm and moved closer. "You look lovely, too, Mr. Corelli," she said. "We should get Jay to take our picture. No one at the office will believe we clean up this well, especially after the sweaty work we've done this week." They had both been constructing display areas and helping haul in lighting fixtures. The entire staff worked manual labor when needed and the money saved poured back into the programs the museum would be able to offer to low-income families.

The wedding ceremony was traditional, using the age-old vows. Along with the requisite 'Love is patient,' verses in I Corinthians, Lincoln had added a scripture passage from Colossians 3. It was one of Carina's favorites.

> *...holy and dearly loved, clothe*
> *yourselves with compassion, kindness,*
> *humility, gentleness, and patience. Bear*
> *with each other and forgive whatever*
> *grievances you may have against one*
> *another. Forgive as the Lord forgave*
> *you. And over all these virtues put on*
> *love, which binds them*
> *all together in perfect unity.*

Philip offered his hand when he saw her wipe away a tear, hoping she couldn't feel his heartbeat when she accepted. Surely everyone around could hear the pounding. He survived the service and sought out Jay as soon as they reached the dining area. "Tell your wife that I'm no longer taking her advice."

"What advice did she offer this time?" Jay asked as he handed Philip a cup of punch. "Where's Carina? You came together, didn't you?"

"Yes, she's finding our seats," he said. "That's the advice I'm talking about. I don't think I'm going to survive the night."

"Do you think she's shutting you out again?" Jay asked. "She just waved and smiled. Are you misinterpreting her actions tonight?"

"No, it's not her, it's me," he said. "Resisting the urge to declare myself in the apartment lobby was difficult enough, but when she held my hand during the ceremony…"

Jay's laughter offered no solace. "Wow, you have it bad, son," he said. "Reminds me of the first time your aunt laughed at one of my lame jokes. I almost proposed on the spot." He saw one brow raise over Philip's tawny eyes. "Not that I'd recommend that, Philip. I guarantee it would ruin everything. You know that, right?"

"Yes," Philip said. "At least I know you have my back."

When Jay shared their conversation with Emilia as they found their place cards, she kissed him soundly. "And people say we women are the sentimental, emotional ones," she said. "Poor Philip."

Poor Philip armed himself with a quick prayer and survived the rest of the evening, able to enjoy their dances with hope. The playful teasing returned, after having disappeared during that fateful car ride. *Hope and be patient. You can do this.*

His resolve was rewarded at her door a few hours later. She wrapped her arms around his waist for a quick hug. "Thank you, Philip. That was a wonderful evening." He trailed his hands down her arms and clasped her hands.

"You're very welcome," he said. He risked a quick kiss on her cheek and let her go. Had he looked back he would have seen her smile as she closed the door.

Chapter 15
Whatever you need

The North Town Ballet Company's production of *Cinderella* was now less than a week away. Carina hadn't mentioned it to anyone at work, other than Philip the few times they discussed her numerous evening activities. The show was Saturday night so rehearsals started earlier and went later than normal. She worked extra hours for several days so that she could take the last half of the week off. A session at the ballet studio followed a mid-morning dentist appointment, but she also found time to work on her ideas for the museum. Mr. Mansfield had agreed to her attending a conference in Panama City after the museum opening. There would be seminars and speakers covering the need for a reemphasis on the arts and discussion talks about ideas for reaching out to underserved communities. She didn't know that Philip had been her most vocal advocate, insisting that the project budget pay for her trip.

Constant activity filled Philip's days that week which was a relief. He'd had no interaction with Carina since the wedding. She was preparing for her days off and he was supervising the finishing touches on the main display areas. The classrooms would be completed later.

Late the night before the performance, he placed a

bouquet of flowers at her door, knowing she'd be home soon. Wording on the card took several attempts, but he finally settled on, 'Praying for you and your performance. I'm honored to be part of your multi-faceted life.'

Sassy provided a running commentary on the way to the city's civic auditorium. "Cinderella is the princess in the story. Her mom is mean," she explained to her cousin, Uncle Philip.

"Stepmom, my dear, not mom," Emmie corrected her daughter.

"Not that it matters, Aunt Emilia," Philip said. "I know some kind stepmoms," he said.

"You're right," Emmie said. "Go on, Sassy, explain the rest of the story to Uncle Philip. He probably doesn't know the story since he only watches boring sports and action movies. Make sure you don't leave out any details."

The shortness of the car ride saved Philip from the full narrative. The magic of the decorated backdrops and scenery quieted the almost five-year old.

Their seats were perfectly situated, close enough to see details but far enough back to be able to see the whole stage. As the hall filled, Philip read the program to Sasha, showing her the places where the ballet would be different from the familiar animated version. He had researched the ballet and understood why the company had chosen this in lieu of Coppelia. Both ballets included roles for younger ballet students, but Cinderella had more humor. "This will be my favorite part," he said, pointing to the 'Fairy Godmother arrives,' scene. Before he could explain, the lights began to dim.

The ballet was beautiful. Sasha had climbed onto her dad's lap to get a better view. When Carina appeared, Emmie reached over and gently lifted Philip's chin that had suddenly dropped. He was mesmerized.

The younger students from local ballet studios filled the roles of mice, garden creatures, and fairies while the older students played additional dancers at the ball. A local seamstress won the contest to design and make the costumes for the students. She had blended the style of the new costumes with the rented costumes used by the main dancers. The sets designed by the college senior stage design class were spectacular. All these details registered vaguely in Philip's mind, but mainly he saw Carina. The Fairy Godmother. Magical, a little bit playful, protective, beautiful, and loving. His heart was no longer his own.

Emilia asked Jay to entertain Sasha during intermission so she could talk to Philip. "Nephew, we've had this conversation before," she said. "Make sure this is real, not infatuation. I'm sure Carina's outer beauty tonight is overwhelming, and we both know and love her inner beauty. Make sure your priorities are in the right order. Wait." Her look stopped him before he began to defend himself. "Listen to me. There's a sadness about her at times, and if you're 'all in' you will need to support her no matter what."

Philip assured her. "I am 'all in,' dear Aunt. I'm waiting now for God's timing…not always patiently, but I'm trying," Philip said. "Yes, she took my breath away tonight, but it wasn't the first time nor will it be the last. Her well-being—physical, emotional, and spiritual—is now more important to me than anything else."

They would both realize soon the timeliness of this conversation.

As the lights rose during the standing ovation, it was a chance for the performers to see the audience. Philip saw Carina's eyes widen when she spotted them. Sasha waved wildly and Carina blew her a kiss. She caught Philip's eye and nodded. As the performers left the stage, Philip sought out an usher. "Yes, you're welcome backstage. The parents of the young performers are all in the banquet hall. The main dancers have private dressing rooms." He recommended waiting fifteen minutes or so for the crowd to thin out.

Philip was almost as impatient as Sasha. The dancer who had portrayed Cinderella was returning from the stage, having spent time with her family there, and she directed them to Carina's room. Emilia knocked on the door. "Carina, your fan club is here. Are you decent?" They heard her laugh as she opened the door.

"If you can call a mismatched outfit decent," she said. Bright red sweatpants were paired with a paint-stained sweatshirt. Sasha jumped into her arms.

"You were magical, Rina! Can I have your autograph?" Carina complied and accepted hugs from Emmie and Jay. Philip waited just inside the door.

"It's a bit crowded in here," Jay said, after rescuing Carina from her youngest fan who was trying on various hats and props found all around the dressing room. "And someone needs to find a restroom. We'll head out to the lobby, Em. Take your time." He winked at Philip before he left.

In the hallway a woman was waiting. "Is this Carina Whitley's dressing room?" Jay nodded and opened the door for her. He stayed long enough to hear the introduction, but not the aftermath.

"Carina?" The middle-aged woman hesitated in the doorway. "I'm Carla Danvers, Doris Booth's daughter. I don't know if you remember me. We only met once."

Philip caught Carina as her knees buckled.

"I'm so sorry to barge in like this, but my mom is very ill and we've been trying to locate you for months. I have a letter from her," she said, her hand shaking as she handed a sealed envelope to Emmie. "I know part of what you went through and it may not mean much, but I'm so sorry for what you suffered. We're not looking for forgiveness, but my mom wanted you to know she recognizes her part in your pain. She's at Emory on the hospice floor, but we understand if you want nothing to do with us. Again, from our whole family, we are sorry."

Tears were running down the woman's face by the time she finished. Emilia escorted her out. "We'll make sure Carina gets home safe," she told the distraught woman.

Philip had lowered Carina onto the couch, moving the props Sasha had played with out of the way. He knelt on the floor next to her. She tensed and swatted his hand away when he tried to brush the hair out of her eyes. She blinked as she stared at him blankly, then the tears started. She sat up suddenly and struggled for breath. He reached for her again and this time she melted into his arms. He was whispering comfort to her when Emmie returned.

"I'm going to carry you to the car," he said. "Is that okay?" She nodded against his chest. With unspoken communication, Emmie followed, texting Jay to take Sasha home, and to pray for Carina. They'd been married long enough for him to accept the simple explanation, *I'll fill you in later.*

Emmie drove, and Philip sat in the back still holding Carina. Hopefully there wouldn't be a traffic stop checking seatbelt usage. Carina had recovered by the time they got to the Philip's apartment. "I'm hungry," she said. "Can you order pizza?"

Philip dialed and placed the order while Emmie scoured his pantry for snacks. She popped a bag of popcorn and poured a soda for Carina. "Eat," she said. "Philip's going to meet the pizza guy downstairs."

"I'm sorry I collapsed," Carina said after a few handfuls of popcorn. "Thank you for rescuing me. After I eat, I'll go back to my apartment."

Maternal Emilia appeared and nixed that idea immediately. "Nope, you're staying here, Philip can sleep on the couch, or we'll send him to your apartment. I'm staying."

"But…" Carina started to object.

"No objections," Emmie said. "I've been eyeing Philip's recliner. It's more comfortable than my bed right now. Jay wanted to invest in a double-wide recliner because he says he can't sleep without me." She sighed.

"He doesn't get it."

The pizza arrived and they discussed the ballet. "You were amazing," Emmie said. "I took one tap class when I was ten years old, and the teacher pulled my mom aside and recommended that we concentrate on soccer instead."

As they finished off the meal, Philip pulled a bag of cookies from their hiding place—having sworn them to secrecy before he shared. He made a pot of coffee and they settled on the living room sofa.

"I suppose you want to know what that was all about," Carina said.

"You owe us no explanation," Philip said. "We're here for you, whatever you need."

"Thank you, but I think it's time I let you both in," Carina said. "I do have a counselor that I've seen for years, but even she told me recently I needed to be more open," she paused, "especially with you, Philip."

They ate cookies and drank coffee in silence for a few minutes. Finally, Carina took a deep breath. "You need to know I've forgiven all those involved, and that I've healed greatly emotionally. Tonight was just a shock. Don't worry that I'm going to endanger myself or fall into a deep depression—not that those responses would be surprising or anything to be ashamed of. God has been so good to me. The healing has been amazing and I understand sharing what I went through and how I've survived can help others. I experienced that in college when I helped a suitemate who had experienced similar mistreatment. It's hard to understand, but being able to help turns the bad times into a blessing."

Carina's story took less than half an hour to share.

Philip and Emilia knew that she left out details, but could imagine what she didn't include.

Her parents had died in a car wreck when she was six years old. Her aunt and uncle were her closest relatives, but were overseas at the time and child protective services had been unable to locate them immediately. Her mom's second cousin lived in a neighboring county and he was named in the will as a temporary guardian if needed. He and her parents weren't close. Carina remembered being at his house several times as a young child, but nothing more.

The cousin died several years before but his widow, Doris, now remarried, took her in. Their only daughter, Clara Danvers, was married and didn't live nearby. Doris Booth's new husband was away often, traveling for business, but his adult son lived in the home. The stepson drank, dabbled in drugs and the usual vices of a young man with no supervision or caring parents.

When he was drinking, he became violent—yelling and throwing things, stumbling around until he passed out. "The noises were terrifying. He would scream and curse his stepmom and she would yell back and then everything would go quiet." She paused, reliving the memories, then continued, her voice quieter. "I heard him talk about 'that brat' turning her into a lazy..." Carina glanced at her friends as she continued. "Well, you can guess what he called his mom. She never spoke of the incidences, or explained her bruises and bandages, but would lock me in my room if he came home obviously under the influence."

When she paused once more, Emmie moved to her

side. "I'm okay," Carina said, "I promise. Sharing my story helps." The six-year-old Carina understood little of what was happening, but instinct caused her to cower and hide whenever the stepson was home. "A silently crying six-year-old forced into their home made an already dysfunctional relationship worse." She missed the look between Philip and Emmie, not realizing she'd failed to mention that she hadn't talked since her parents' accident.

"I don't know for sure," Carina said, "but I think Mrs. Booth's daughter Carla knew about the physical and verbal abuse, because she never came to visit her mom. I only met her when Mrs. Booth took me with her to visit them. Mother and daughter argued, she remembered, and now knew it was likely about the stepson.

Emmie squeezed her hand, sensing the worst of the story approaching. She glanced at her nephew, saw a clenched jaw, and balled fists. Her warning glance forced him to relax as Carina finished.

The stepson gambled heavily, too, and the final event was when he owed a lot of money to some dangerous people. "I was supposed to be at a birthday party at a neighbor's house, but the family cancelled it due to a chicken pox outbreak. Frustrated that she didn't have the afternoon free from me, Mrs. Booth ranted and told me to stay in my room. She didn't know her stepson had planned to use the opportunity of an empty house to look for money. He was furious when he got home. I hid under my bed, out of some surreal instinct. After he confronted his mom, he rifled through my bedroom. His addictions and panic over his debts clouded his thinking and he thought his mom hid the money in the least likely place."

During her story recounting that night, Carina pulled her legs up, and wrapped her arms around her knees. "I think I made myself fall asleep." Her voice trailed off. "The next thing I remember is a young female police officer whispering, "It's okay, sweetie. I've got you."

Philip grabbed a blanket and tucked it around her. His presence seemed to surprise Carina as she blinked away the fog of memories.

Philip took a chance and reached for her. "The money?" he asked, finally breaking his silence as she leaned against him.

"Emergency funds from the church initially, and later from social services money that came with the arrangement for the Booths to take me in," she said. "I didn't find out about it until years later and finally understood why he thought there was money in my room."

Carina straightened up and smiled at her new confidantes. "But God was good. Mrs. Booth put aside her fear of the consequences and called 911. The police raided the house, and within minutes I was bundled up and taken straight to the hospital. I stayed with a church family for a couple weeks until my aunt and uncle returned to the States."

The trio sat silently for several minutes, then Emmie sprang into action. "Philip, go make sure your room is clean. Carina's staying here tonight," Emmie said. "I'm claiming the recliner. You can go to her apartment, my house, or take the couch." Carina didn't protest, knowing it would be fruitless. Emmie followed her to her apartment where she took a quick shower and put on over-sized sweatshirt and sweatpants, her usual after-performance outfit. Back in Philip's apartment she apologized to him for ruining his dress shirt.

"Stage makeup is impossible to get out of clothes," she said. "I'll buy you a new one."

"No need," Philip said as he showed her into his room. "There are extra blankets on the chair. I need to run out for a little bit, but Emmie will be right in the living room. Okay?" Carina nodded drowsily. "Goodnight, Carina."

"Goodnight, Philip," she said as she crawled into his bed. "Thank you for taking care of me."

"You're welcome, dear." He tucked the covers around her, then waited by the door. She was asleep within minutes.

In the kitchen, Emilia watched her nephew, knowing his emotions were simmering just below the surface.

"There's more to this," Philip said as they cleaned up the pizza remnants. "A trip to the hospital when the police rescued her, and the protection—weak as it was—that Mrs. Booth put into place tells me that he hurt Carina, too. Maybe only once, but he did, I'm sure. Her rescue before he could do more doesn't mediate my anger at the danger she was in."

"You're probably correct, but we have to trust Carina to share when she's ready, if ever, and love her no matter what."

"That's a given," he said.

"Where are you going?" Emmie asked as Philip grabbed his duffel bag from the hall closet.

"Lincoln's picking me up to go get Carina's car," he

said. "Then I'm going to the all-night gym. If I don't hit something soon, in a legitimate environment, I may be in danger of hurting the first shady character I run into."

Philip slept on the couch and got up before the ladies. He checked in on Carina, heartbroken as he watched her sleep. Emmie woke soon after and called Jay to give him an update. She'd called him late last night and didn't give details, but shared enough to let him know why she was staying. Her husband had wisely asked how Philip was doing. "I can imagine the anger and helplessness. Tell him I'm praying for both him and Carina."

The fresh aroma of coffee woke their guest. Carina appeared in the bedroom doorway. "Something smells delicious."

"Are you hungry?" Philip asked. "I'm cooking."

"Please tell me it's not scrambled eggs and orange juice," she said as she joined him in the kitchen to pour herself a cup of coffee.

"Once again, you're hilarious," he said. The eeriness of acting normal after last night, was both comforting and confusing, but he was glad the teasing hadn't disappeared. He knew she'd had years to deal with the trauma. He had to trust that she knew she was safe and would continue to let him into her life.

Over pancakes and bacon she shared what was in the letter Carla had given her. "I didn't read it until this morning. Mrs. Booth wrote it several years ago, so it's a bit cryptic. Basically, she admits that she could've protected me but was so enamored with her new husband that she didn't want to cause trouble. She thought the money that my care generated would help their marriage.

His continued and more frequent absences after I left led to her drink more, and he was physically abusive when he was home. They divorced over ten years ago. Her stepson spent several years in jail, then she lost track of him. He died recently, she heard through another relative."

As she helped with the breakfast dishes, which she did despite Philip's protest, she said, "I'm going to go visit her in the hospital this afternoon."

"I'm going with you," Philip said.

"Not necessary. I'll be fine, really." She rearranged the clean dishes for a third time, and mumbled under her breath. "I can do this."

"Don't argue, Carina," Emilia said. "Please! I'll have to deal with his pouting if you don't let him go."

"Fine," she said. "I'll be ready in half an hour." Hugging Emmie before she left to return to her apartment, she whispered, "Thank you, my friend."

The trip to the hospital took a little over an hour. Philip kept the conversation to museum business. The opening was a month away, so their days would be frenzied. Checking the rest of the Mansfield collection for any needed repairs was the largest task left, but Philip hired a professional appraiser since he'd be overseeing the finishing of the physical building, writing the descriptions, and checking the graphic designer's layouts for the catalog. All the final preparations for the opening gala fell to Carina. Although the board approved a complete children's program for the museum, its launch would have to wait until the beginning of summer, if not later. Her disappointment was tempered by her upcoming conference trip.

As they parked in the hospital's multi-level garage, Philip offered her his arm. "Are you sure you're up to this, Carina?"

"Honestly, no, but I need to do it," she said, moving closer as they walked. "I know I said you didn't need to come, but I'm glad you're here."

The doctors had started a heavier dose of pain meds so Mrs. Booth was asleep when they arrived. A weepy Carla thanked them for coming. They visited with her for almost an hour as she asked about Carina's life and described the new life her mom had led over the last few years. She left briefly for an update from the nurse. When she returned, she said, "The doctors said Mom will sleep most of the rest of the day, but when she wakes up, I'll let her know you were here."

"Thank you for reaching out to me," Carina said. "I had forgiven it all many years ago, but it's good to have some more closure. I'll pray for your mom and your whole family."

Carina treated Philip to her favorite Atlanta eatery, The Varsity, before they headed back. "You can't come to Atlanta and not eat here," she said around a juicy mouthful of hotdog.

Feeling the relief of closure, Carina filled in some of the missing pieces to her story while they ate.

Within days of the accident, six-year-old Carina had to help decide what to pack for herself for the weeks before her aunt and uncle arrived. One of the church families, with children who were her closest friends, gathered mementos and family photo albums and filled a large chest for her to take with her, not knowing how long it would be before her relatives arrived.

One of the church elders was a lawyer and had advised her parents to appoint the pastor as executor of their will when their closest relatives were moving overseas. The church family helped with all the legal issues and many of the decisions her aunt and uncle faced when they returned. After lengthy discussions, they decided to sell the house and move out of the area. "They had an apartment in Washington, but now needed a permanent home. I remember a lot of our furnishings in the new home were from my house, which helped with my transition."

"Unfortunately, the chest of mementos disappeared somehow," Carina said. "After I left the Booth's house, contact with them was limited for my safety. Not that they'd be willing to look for it." She squeezed Philip's hand when she felt him tense. "Relax, friend. I'm fine. The pastor stored several huge boxes of keepsakes, my mom's wedding dress, and all sorts of important stuff, in his attic."

She didn't pull away when he laced his fingers with hers. "I've moved them with me everywhere. They're in a storage unit. Whenever I find a house, I'll have an unpacking party." Needing to lighten the atmosphere, she added, "Maybe that young realtor could help me look for one."

"Not funny, ma'am," Philip said. He had recently confessed the real reason the young assistant realtor had been called away. "Let's hit the road. You can practice your comedy routine on the way home. You'll need to be on your game when my family gets here." The opening gala coincided with Easter and Sasha's birthday so the family planned an impromptu reunion. Philip's sister and brother would drive down on Saturday morning with his grandparents.

The comedy practice lost out to fatigue. "I'm stuffed," Carina said. Philip had insisted they share a chocolate shake to complete their meal. As they reached the edge of downtown, she yawned. "I'm sleepy. Will you be okay if I nap?"

"Of course," he said and turned the volume down on the radio. "I'll nudge you if you start snoring."

"Ha, ha," she said as she grabbed the jacket he'd tossed in the back seat. She leaned her seat back and was asleep in minutes. Philip prayed, with his eyes open literally and his heart open spiritually.

My heart is aching. Your ways are so far above the understanding of mere men, but the evil in the world, and the evil directed at this precious lady, makes me so angry that I'm struggling to accept it. Why? Why her? Why after she suffered such a loss was this added? Why does this happen? Lord, I'm asking for your peace, for your justice, your vengeance. Thank you for the example that Carina has shown me, the resilience, the forgiveness, the ability to see that You can even turn tragedy to good. Her seeing Your glory, mercy and grace is humbling. Thank you for bringing her into our lives. Please help me not get ahead of Your plans. Help me love her well, in whatever form is Your will.

Chapter 16
Don't panic...keep talking

When Mira received an unexpected call the Monday after Carina's ballet performance she cleared her schedule. "Let's meet for lunch," she suggested to Carina. It didn't take long for Carina to describe what had happened, and Mira was pleased at how her patient handled the reopening of long-healed wounds. Losing your parents at six years old, and then landing in an abusive situation, left deep scars, but Carina's faith and family support offered a deeper healing. "I'm proud that you let Philip and Emilia comfort you. It was a huge step," she said. "Sharing the burden with someone else, especially someone that cares for you as much as they obviously do, will go a long way to deeper healing." They finished their meal and stood on the sidewalk and Mira had a few more insights, "Have you called your aunt and uncle yet?"

"Yes," Carina said, "late last night. The time difference worked in my favor for once. I knew they were disappointed not being able to make the ballet, but there was an airline workers strike in Europe that cancelled their flight. They feel doubly guilty now for not being there, but I think I was able to convince them this was a good thing."

"I'm glad you see it that way," Mira said. Knowing Carina's emotional journey would be a lifelong one, though, she added a mild warning. "You may have a setback suddenly, even over the next few weeks. Don't panic. Keep talking. Let them know what's going on." When Carina gave her a hug, she whispered, "And by them, I mean your family *and* Philip."

The next three weeks were hectic, which helped distract Carina. Final preparations, advertising, guest lists and checking on the caterers, florists, and musicians scheduled for the opening gala filled the long hours. Carina put her volunteer activities on hold, using her small amount of free time to work on her proposals for the children's programs. Experts at the upcoming conference offered opportunities for attendees to bring in their plans to get feedback. Once the board approved her preliminary suggestions for the children's activities, Carina scheduled an appointment as soon as the slots opened.

As the pace of preparations sped up, Mr. Mansfield scheduled twice weekly staff meetings to ensure that the project stayed on track. At the first meeting after the ballet, Philip slid into the seat next to her and slipped her a note. '*Are you good?*'

She took the note and added her response, '*Only when required.*' His guffaw drew a frown from Mr. Mansfield. Their good behavior lasted through the next meeting that week but only because Philip had to leave early to receive a delivery at the warehouse. Philip cleared his morning schedule so he could be at the meeting early. It was one of the few times he knew for sure he'd see Carina. He chose a seat out of Mr.

Mansfield's line of sight, but with a clear view of Carina.

Before this meeting, Garrett Mansfield's normally calm personality showed signs of stress. Carina made sure he had his hot tea and Danish well before the meeting so by the time it started, his optimism returned, and even added a bit of humor. "Carina informs me that everything's on or ahead of schedule. According to her, Mr. Corelli was an excellent hire. He apparently knows what he's doing." Carina glanced at Philip and realized her mistake too late. He winked broadly. Her phone slipped off her lap as she aimed a kick his way.

Mr. Mansfield turned to her. "Are you all right, Miss Whitley?"

"Yes, yes sir," she said. "Here's the guest list. The affirmatives are highlighted." She glared at Philip as he rescued her phone and tugged it away before she could grab it. "Stop it," she whispered. Thankfully, Mr. Mansfield missed the interchange as her perused the list.

Now, over a week and a half later, Philip seized the opportunity for a longer, more private conversation. Late in the afternoon, a few days before opening, he met Carina in the parking lot. "I can't believe it. She's real!"

"Who?" Carina faked confusion, looking behind her.

"The illusive Ree-Rina-Carina Whitley," he said, holding the door open for her and relieving her of half the load of bags. "How have you been, my friend? I know it's been torture not driving me to work and not having me dog your footsteps through the office."

"True, although your antics in the staff meetings almost got both of us fired. Remember?" She unlocked her car. "I hear you've been annoying the decorators and interns at the warehouse," Carina said. "Spreading the love around, I see."

I don't think that means what you think that means, he thought. Out loud, he chose his words more wisely, "Seemed only fair to me." He helped her load the bags into the back seat. "What's in these?"

"Supplies to make the party favors for the children," she said. "Although the children's activities won't be starting until the fall, there will be children at the opening. One of the classrooms is complete enough that we've hired a couple interns to hang out and help the kids make their own artwork." She turned to him, brows furrowed. "Aren't you the Head Curator? Didn't you know we were doing this?"

"I heard rumors, but Mr. Mansfield told me it was 'Carina's baby,' so I knew it was in good hands."

Philip reached into one of the bags and pulled out a small set of watercolors. "What are you doing with these?" He opened the next bag. It had watercolor pencils and brushes.

"Stop it!" Carina pulled his hand away. "You're such a child. You could've simply asked me what was in the bags."

"I did," he said as he placed the last bag on the floorboard and closed the door. "If these are the party favors, why are you taking them home?"

"As I said, these are the supplies for the party favors. I still have to put the sets together," she said. "You know, like a gift bag for a kid's birthday party."

"How many of these do you have to make?" Philip's evening priorities suddenly changed as opportunity presented itself. He held open the driver's side door. "Do you want some help?" When she didn't answer, he bent down while she buckled her seat belt. "C'mon, Carina. You know you miss me."

"Do I?" She let him close the door, but rolled down the window. "I know you've been a little preoccupied. I hear there's something big going on this week with your job."

"That's true, but I'll always have time to help out a friend," he said. "Especially when I know she'd order pizza and bake cookies to pay me for my help."

"You want to spend your evening making party favors for kids?"

With you, absolutely, his thoughts speaking truthfully again. "Yes, of course. I live for making party favors."

Carina glanced at the supplies in her back seat. Left alone, she'd be up until midnight or later. "Okay. Give me half an hour to get it organized," she said, adding as she started her engine, "I'll take sausage and green onions on my pizza."

By the Philip arrived with the pizza, Carina had placed the supplies around her dining room table, preheated the oven and taken the cookie dough out of the freezer. The last time she made cookies for their Bible study group, she'd doubled the recipe and frozen half.

They ate their pizza while Carina described how she planned to assemble the favors which included a small set of watercolors, a brush, watercolor pencils, and a set of artist trading cards featuring famous masterpieces wrapped in a scroll of watercolor paper, and tied with a ribbon. After several comical attempts, Carina admitted she'd been foolish to think she could do this by herself.

"I'd be here until next week," she said. "This is definitely a two-person job."

Philip's sense of order rescued them. "You stack, I'll wrap, you tie the ribbon." The plan worked. They worked steadily, only taking a break for coffee and cookies.

"I know we have a caterer for the gala, but I wish we'd have you make these cookies for it," Philip said as he stuffed another one in his mouth. "These are delicious."

"Don't talk with your mouth full," she said. "Thank you for the endorsement. I'll clear my schedule so I can make forty dozen cookies in my spare time between now and, let me think…oh yes…two days from now."

They spent the evening catching up. His days at the warehouse turned museum had been long, and Carina had worked almost exclusively in her office which was still in the college building. Carina asked how Philip felt the museum preparations were going, which he said were running smoothly. He asked about the responses to the invitations and was surprised at how many people were expected.

"You've had over a hundred responses? We might want to hire a few more people for next week's public opening." He pulled out his phone and added to his to-do list.

After a break in the conversation, Carina broached

the subject she knew was on his mind. "I'm doing fine, Philip," she said. "Don't ever be afraid to ask. If I'm not ready to share, I'll let you know." She put down her coffee mug and placed her hand on his forearm. He covered it with his, then lifted it to his lips. He hesitated but when she smiled, he kissed it gently.

"You do have someone you talk to professionally, don't you?" He asked. "Is that one of the places you disappear to regularly?"

"Yes, I do, and yes, it is." Carina said. "I've been blessed with the same counsellor since I was eleven or twelve. She even moved to this area recently—not specifically for me, but it was definitely a gift. I hadn't talked to her in a couple years until recently."

"After the ballet?" Philip asked, as he washed opened another pack of trading cards.

"No, before that," Carina said. She paused, giving him a chance to decide his next move.

"May I ask why?"

"It was because of you," she said.

He paled. "Carina, I'm so sorry. Tell me what I did," he dried his hands quickly and reached for hers. She bit her lip—he assumed in distress. "I never meant to hurt you in any way. Emmie tells me all the time that I'm clueless when it comes to women, but I thought I had gotten better, but I guess not. What did I do?"

Carina stopped his rambling as she let a laugh escape. "I'm sorry Philip for laughing, but you're so cute. No, you've been nothing but a kind, caring friend, and gentleman." She squeezed his hands before turning him back to their project. "I called her because my reaction to you confused me."

"Confused you?" Philip asked. "Your reaction to me?"

"Yes," she said. "You made it easy for me to trust you, quicker than I'd ever experienced. My lack of concern over my confusion made it even more confusing." She laughed as he processed her circular reasoning. "Welcome to my brain," she said. "Basically, my wise counsellor told me to relax, although she worded it more diplomatically."

He took the unfinished craft from her hands and turned her toward him. "Thank you for trusting me. I know now may not be the time, but we need to have a serious talk about this," he said, pointing to himself and then touching her nose. "Soon. I'm tired of keeping what I feel for you quiet. Understood?"

She nodded, then whispered, "Me, too."

"Now, back to work, young lady," Philip said.

They finished the favors by ten, earlier than expected, but Carina was already yawning. Her day had started early again with a quick ballet work out at the studio. Philip washed the coffee mugs while she repacked the unused supplies. At the door, she handed him a box containing the remaining cookies. "Thank you, Philip," she said.

When he placed the box on the shelf by the door, she didn't hesitate as he opened his arms. He savored the moment as held her close. "Thank *you*, Carina." He kissed her forehead and added, "Sleep well."

Chapter 17
No, I'm not afraid

Thanks to another girls' shopping trip, Carina had the perfect outfit for the opening gala. Knowing she'd be checking on the children's area periodically, and would likely be called to help the young artists, she chose comfort over style. Tess's suggestion of a stylish jumpsuit paired with low heels proved helpful. The dark blue and colorful floral pattern flattered Carina's fair coloring and the style allowed the movement needed to corral any unruly children.

At the end of the day, Carina discovered why Tess had pushed for her outfit's color choice. Her sly friend kept saying, "This is the perfect color. I promise." The cryptic remarks made sense now. On her counter was a small box with a label from the ski lodge. Inside were the earrings she had seen in the gift shop. The blue topaz dangles matched the pantsuit exactly. She started to call Tess to thank her, wondering how she could've afforded them. What stopped her was the note underneath the box. *'Here's to a great grand opening...and thanks for putting up with me. Sincerely yours, Philip.'* Had it not been so late, she would've headed to his apartment to thank him personally. She settled for a text.

'You will have to explain the levels of intrigue that went into accomplishing this. You shouldn't have, but I

know you well enough that I can hear you defending yourself. Thank you, Philip. This means more than I'm able to express. ~Carina'

An hour before the official party, Mr. Mansfield planned a staff-only meeting in the front of the museum for the official unveiling of the Winfield Museum sign. Philip thanked the staff for all their hard work before relinquishing the podium to his boss.

"I've been reminded that we still have a party to prep for so I'll keep my comments short," Garrett Mansfield promised, with the caveat, "if I can. No promises." Their director's self-deprecation drew laughter, but had always garnered respect and devotion from the staff.

Carina smiled at Philip when he reached her side. "Nice earrings," he said. "Are you ready? This is exciting, isn't it?" When he reached for her hand, hiding the touch from their colleagues, she didn't resist.

"You look quite handsome, Mr. Corelli," she said. "I'm sorry I won't be available to defend you from the onslaught."

"Onslaught?" Philip asked, keeping his voice low. "What onslaught?"

"The ladies, dear Philip," she giggled as she released his hand. "Launch a flare if you get overwhelmed."

Before he could respond, Mr. Mansfield called him back to the podium. "Here's Philip to do the honors," he said. A tug on the rope, and the sign was revealed. The graphic design department's contest gave the board several notable choices for the logo. Everyone agreed the winning design captured both the heritage of the Mansfield name and the vision for the future brought by the Winston college community. Philip thanked the staff once more, then sent them off to get ready for the guests due to arrive soon.

Carina waved to Philip and gave him a 'thumbs up' before heading inside to check on the children's area. They crossed paths a few more times during the evening, once at the refreshment table. "This reminds me of the fundraiser," he said as he filled a plate for her.

"You know me well," she said as he picked all her favorites. "The evening is a success, I think. The children's area has been a big hit, which is encouraging." Philip only managed a nod since he'd just stuffed an entire lobster roll into his mouth. She reached to wipe the cream from his chin. "You're a mess, sweetheart."

"I haven't eaten since breakfast," he said after taking a long drink of punch. He glanced towards the desserts at the end of the table. "Do you have cookies in the kids' room? Nothing down there looks appetizing." She promised to save him one, or four, before seeing one of the interns waving for her from the classroom.

"I'm being summoned," she said. She brushed imaginary crumbs from his lapel. "Behave if you can."

"No promises," he said, devouring a bacon pinwheel in one bite. "Go rescue the helpers. I'll let you know when my family gets here. They're looking forward to meeting you."

When Sasha dragged her dad into the children's classroom, Carina knew the family had arrived. "Hello Rina," Sasha tugged her friend's hand. "My Auntie

June and Uncle Mark are here. C'mon!"

"Alexandra June! Miss Carina is working. She'll come hang out with us when she can." Jay smiled in apology. "Look, sweetheart," he steered the youngster toward the art projects. "You can stay here and make your own artwork. Doesn't that sound like fun?"

"Can Rina help me?"

"Sure, I can," Carina said, "if it's okay with your dad. The project doesn't take but a few minutes, Jay, then we'll come find you."

Two minutes later Philip appeared at the door of the classroom. "Here you are, Sassy! Auntie June and Uncle Mark wanted to see the children's area."

"Uncle Philip, look what I'm doing! Rina's helping me!" Sasha held up her partially completed watercolor.

Philip admired the painting and winked at Carina, "This is awesome, Sassy," he said. "Go ahead and finish while I talk to Carina."

Carina grabbed a baby wipe, cleaned her hands, and untied her art apron while Philip and his parents admired the completed paintings now displayed around the room. When she checked in with the interns, confirming that they had control of the activities, she joined him.

"Carina Whitley, these are my parents, June and Mark," he said. "They asked me to apologize for any and all of my misbehavior since we met. It was not their fault, although Emilia has some stories about my mom that she's promised to tell me."

"All pure fiction, I'm sure," June Corelli said. "Carina, it's so nice to meet you. This is wonderful. Philip said the children's programs are your brainchild. Tell me more." She slipped her arm through Carina's and led her out to the main room. Philip and his dad followed after assuring Sasha that her parents were coming to get her in a minute.

Before they reached the ladies, his dad elbowed him, "Carina? If what Emmie and Jay have told us, we're thrilled. She seems delightful." His son's grin told his dad all he needed to know.

Carina introduced the Corellis to Mr. and Mrs. Mansfield and the other board members. Professor Patel joined them as they admired the modern art collection, June Corelli's favorite section. She and her husband spent the rest of the evening with the professor and Carina. Philip's parents showed genuine interest in her plans for reaching the community with opportunities to enjoy and create art.

"She's our champion," Professor Patel said. "We're excited to see the projects she has planned come to fruition."

As they reached the dessert buffet, Carina excused herself and checked in with the caterer. Before she could rejoin Philip, Mr. Mansfield motioned her over to his group. She stopped and thanked the Corellis for coming. "It was so nice meeting you," she said. "You've raised an honorable, kind man. Thank you for sharing him." Her simple words were meant for his parents' ears only, but Philip had come around the corner of the column that had hidden him from her view. He stepped back before she spotted him.

"Well, son," his dad asked later when they were alone. "Is there anything you need to tell us?"

Philip understood the unspoken questions. "Yes, she's amazing, yes I've fallen in love with her, but no," he said, "I don't think she has any idea."

Jay and Philip's dad stayed to help clean up. They, along with Philip, appeared at the door of the children's classroom. Suit coats and vests gone, ties loosened, sleeves rolled up, they stood with hands on their hips. "You look like a group of bizarrely uniformed foot soldiers or a nerdy boy band," Carina said. Her comments generated a fierce, but hilarious debate over which would be the lead singer in the band and which one was more qualified to lead troops.

"Have you heard my dad sing?" Philip asked Jay. "I can at least carry a tune."

"But I'm a firefighter," Jay said, "of course I'd be the front guy for the band. You guys have seen our calendars, right?"

Thankfully, the teasing didn't stop their usefulness. Of course, the usefulness also didn't stop their teasing. Whenever they were within earshot of Carina, Jay and Philip's dad took turns telling embarrassing stories about Philip. Carina hadn't laughed so hard in years. "Stop, please," she said. "It's almost midnight. If you two don't stop we'll never finish."

"I agree," Philip said. "I also demand equal time. At Easter dinner, I get to tell Carina about that one time that you two…" His father stopped him mid-sentence.

"Whoa there, son," he said, "we have work to do. Let's not get distracted!"

"Easter dinner?" Carina asked as she handed him the box for the left-over supplies. "Did I miss something?"

Philip apologized. "I thought Emmie had asked you already. I know you're coming to Sassy's birthday party on Monday. She made it clear that you were invited when she heard our boss had given us the day off. Can you join us for Easter dinner? The rest of the family arrives tomorrow, so they'll be here for church and Sassy's birthday party." He finished packing the box and stacked it with the others. "I have to warn you, though. You've only seen a small snippet of the craziness." He saw her pensive look and tried to ease what he thought was concern or fear. Lifting her off the floor where she was collecting dropped brushes and papers, he swept a loose curl behind her ear. "I know it sounds scary, but I promise to protect you if it's overwhelming."

She blinked at him and shook her head. "No, I'm not afraid," she said as she tugged his tie, pulling him closer. "I love your family," Carina whispered.

He brushed a kiss on her cheek. "The feeling is mutual," he said.

On Saturday morning, Emilia called, inviting Carina to the annual egg dyeing extravaganza. "Please come. Philip's heading down the hall to ask you, but I accidently let it slip to Sasha and now she'll be super disappointed if you don't come."

"No pressure, right? A little more notice would've helped, ma'am," she said, glancing at her baggy workout pants and old t-shirt. Carina hesitated, but not long enough to think of reasons not to go before she heard Philip's knock. "He's here, but I'm not promising anything. I may or may not be there today, but I am looking forward to tomorrow."

"That's fair," Emmie said, knowing Philip wouldn't take 'no' easily.

"Hello, Philip," she said as she opened the door. "So,

I'm being summoned to spend the day with your family—people I just met, by the way. Perhaps I have a full schedule of chores planned."

"Do you?" he asked.

"Yes," she said, "as you can see by my lovely outfit. Now you expect me to shower, change clothes and put up with you on a non-work Saturday? You have one minute to convince me. Go."

"First," he said. "Ouch. Spending the day with me goes in the 'con' column?" When she nodded, he pouted, but undeterred he continued. "One minute? Plenty of time," he said. "Sassy, cookies, coloring eggs at an 'eggstravaganza' beyond any you can imagine. Done."

Carina hadn't colored eggs since elementary school. Her Easter memories from before her parents died included her mom's penchant for trying new techniques every year and her dad's insistence that he was 'too old for this,' as he joined in, proudly sending photos of his work to several co-workers. She glanced at Philip as he leaned casually against her open door.

"Well?" he asked. When Carina didn't respond, he pulled out his phone. "Here, I'll call Sassy."

Carina grabbed his phone. "No, I'll go," she said, handing it back to him. "Give me ten minutes. I'll meet you downstairs."

Five hours and three dozen eggs later, Philip drove Carina home. It had been a lively time with Jay and Philip's antics reminding her of her father. She declined to play judge when they debated whose eggs were decorated best. Philip lobbied for his, using his background in art as his reason for her to pick his.

"You have an art background?" Carina asked. "Wow,

I never suspected that." Her sarcasm won her hoots of approval from Jay and Philip's dad. She shoved a cookie in his open mouth to prevent his rebuttal.

She took a photo of her half dozen eggs, each reflecting her love of watercolors and Monet. Posting it on her own social media brought a wave of sadness. She shook it off leaning instead on the laughs and fellowship of the day. Philip's parents were delightful. The sisters were close despite the difference in their ages, and they welcomed Carina into their circle of friendship.

Philip's siblings and grandparents were later than expected due to traffic delays, and arrived as the 'eggstravaganza' ended. As promised, Philip took Carina home before dinner, but her brief interaction with his grandparents, Cassandra and Gino, cemented their approval for their brother's new relationship. "We'll fill her in on your faults tomorrow," Cassandra warned her brother. "Hopefully, she'll still have you. She's wonderful."

Saturday night Carina called to video chat with Mira. Her counselor was also an art enthusiast, so she wanted to hear about the grand opening. Carina eagerly shared how well the event went, but didn't mention the day's activity, or the plans for Easter dinner. Still, Mira noticed how often Philip's name came up.

"Sounds like the closeness with Philip continues," Mira said. "How do you feel about that?"

"I'm not sure," Carina said. "I thought it would scare me, but it doesn't. Still, am I ready to acknowledge that it's a real relationship?"

Mira smiled. "I want to try an exercise we haven't done before. It may help you."

"Sure," Carina said.

"I'm going to give you two words—they'll be related. I want you to choose one instantly, no overthinking your answer," she said. "Okay?"

"Yes," Carina said, "I guess."

"Tea or Coffee?"

"Coffee," Carina answered.

"High heels or sneakers?"

"Sneakers."

"Cookies or brownies?"

"Yes." Carina laughed.

"I'll give you that one," Mira said. "I wouldn't be able to choose one either. Next one."

"Mozart or Tchaikovsky?"

"Tchaikovsky."

"Sleeping Beauty or Cinderella?" Mira asked and Carina's answer surprised her.

"That's easy," Carina said, "Sleeping Beauty."

"Didn't you dance in a production of Cinderella recently?"

"Yes, but I love the Sleeping Beauty story better."

"Understood," Mira said. "Only a few more. Sunrise or sunset?"

"Sunrise."

"Mountains or the beach?"

"Mountains."

"Carina or Philip?"

"Philip," Carina said, then gasped. "Wait, what? Me or Philip? What do you mean?"

"So, are you sure you don't view this 'whatever-it-is' between you and Philip as a real relationship?" Mira pressed her. "Could you see yourself saying you love him?"

"I'm not sure," Carina said. "I think so."

"Do you?"

"Love him?" Carina asked. "Maybe?"

Mira smiled. "Are those real doubts or are they the 'I'm hiding from a deeper relationship' doubts?"

"Ouch," Carina said. "You're good at this counseling thing, you know."

"Have a great time at the conference next week," Mira said. "The time away will be helpful."

Chapter 18
Do you think she knows?

An early Sunday morning call to her aunt and uncle made for a joyful start to Carina's Easter. Lynette and Clark's European trip was ending soon and they eagerly described the cathedral where they had worshipped that morning. "It was spectacular, dearest. The newly refinished frescos took my breath away," her aunt said, "and I had to hold your uncle's hand the whole way out of the cathedral after the service. He wanted to touch everything."

"It was all so shiny," Clark Whitley said. "But, the service was humbling, too, Carina. Even though we understood few of the words, worshipping the same Lord in a different culture is comforting."

The rest of the conversation centered on the opening events and Carina's weekend plans. Although she tried to downplay the role Philip's family played in her plans, she didn't fool her aunt or uncle. "We're looking forward to meeting your young man in person," Uncle Clark said. "From all you've told us, he sounds like a godly man that respects and cares for you."

Carina was thankful their call was not a video chat this morning, because she knew they'd comment on her blushing. "From all I've told you? I don't remember telling you that much about him." *I'm glad my conversations with Mira are confidential,* she thought.

Her aunt laughed. "Carina, dearest," she said. "We know you well. This man has captured your attention, if not your heart. Your uncle and I want you to know we approve and are here to support you however you, and Philip, decide to move forward."

"Well, this is an ominous ending to our Easter call," Carina said, but tempered her comment with humor. "Speaking of Philip, which apparently is your favorite topic now, he'll be here in a few minutes. We're carpooling to church since there will be limited parking at the Lazlo's house afterwards. I can't wait to see you two in a few weeks." When they returned to the states, they planned to stop at Carina's for a few days before they settled back into their home. The entire family would be together at the July reunion. She assured them that those plans were coming together, too. "I made hotel reservations for the family and Mr. Mansfield said we can use the museum conference space for our dinner if I can't find an outdoor space where we can cook out."

"Sounds good, dear. We love you! Have fun today," her uncle said. "Give Philip our love." He hung up before she could respond, but she was sure she heard her aunt laughing in the background.

In their hotel room half a world away, Lynette Whitley was both laughing and shaking her finger at her husband. "That wasn't very nice, sir," she said. "Do you think she knows?"

"That we've talked to Philip several times without her," he asked, "or that she's head over heels in love with him? Neither, I think," he added. "At least not yet."

Minutes later Philip knocked on the door. Carina called him in. "Door's open and coffee's on," she said. He prepared both their drinks while she found her shoes. Philip found her habit of leaving shoes anywhere but in her closet adorable. "It used to drive my roommates crazy," she had told him when he observed the pile by the door one day. "I can't tell you how many times I was almost late for class because they had put my shoes back in the closet."

On the way to church, Philip asked how her aunt and uncle were doing. "Did they get a chance to go to a church service this morning?" Carina frowned and Philip realized his mistake. Trying to cover his blunder, he added, "You did talk to them this morning? You told me you talk to them a lot, I just assumed..." His ruse apparently satisfied Carina because she answered his question, briefly summarizing her family's cathedral experience.

As they pulled into the church parking lot, Philip saw Carina begin to fiddle with her bracelet. He'd learned the signs of her anxiety over the last few weeks. He turned off the car and reached for her hand. He thought the time with his family yesterday would have eased her nerves, but her silence said otherwise.

"How much do they know, Philip?"

"Nothing, Carina," he said. "Your story is not mine, or Emilia's, to tell." When she nodded, he added, "Of course, they know I've met a wonderful, silly, highly intelligent, although rationally suspect, young lady that I am very excited for them to meet."

"Rationally suspect?" Carina laughed. "Because I like you?"

"Yes, exactly," he said, relieved that her calm—and humor—had returned. "Stay put. I'll come around and get you. My dad may be watching." He winked at her. As he helped her out, he pulled her closer. "You said you liked me. Do you? Like me? Truly?"

She poked his ribs. "Sort of. I guess. A little. If I must."

Emmie and Philip planned to flank her during the church service, but Carina waved Cassandra over to sit with her. Philip winked at Emmie who responded with a wide grin. Jay whispered to his wife. "Behave."

A delicious dinner, tons of family stories, and a surprising lack of personal questions made Carina's afternoon at the Lazlo's delightful. Emilia packed her a plate of leftovers and hugged her warmly as she prepared to leave. "Thank you for putting up with the foolishness. We'll see you tomorrow, which is likely to be just as wild, but on a whole different five-year-old level," Emmie said. As the grown boys chose that moment to start a rock-paper-scissors match replete with trash talk and mocking, she added, "Or maybe not."

The ride back to the apartment gave little opportunity for Philip to debrief because Emmie called Carina to ask if she had an idea for a pinata. The unicorn one she had ordered didn't arrive and Philip's mom checked three stores and nobody had anything close. "Help! June called from the last store and there are no cute pinatas anywhere. What can I do?"

Carina assured her that she'd think of something.

"Don't worry. I've already got a couple of ideas swimming around in my head. I'll check the supplies I have at home and call you back in a bit," she said. "The theme is princesses and unicorns, correct?"

"Yes, technically The Unicorn Kingdom, thanks to my nephew," Emmie said with a little annoyed huff.

"Make Philip help you," Emmie said. "He owes me since he's the author of the story. Don't tell him, but it's excellent—not the usual nonsense he makes up. I've even thought about asking my sister to do some illustrations and get it printed for Sassy one Christmas."

An hour later, Philip stood staring at the brightly decorated castle on Carina's kitchen counter. "How did you do that?" he asked as he held it still for her to add the candy.

"Easy peasy," she said. "You were here, remember? It's boxes, paper towel rolls, some paint, and some stickers. I'll go outside in the morning to add the glitter. Unless you'd be willing to let me use your apartment tonight?"

"Tempting," he said, "but no. The Glitter Glam movement hasn't made it into my décor style yet."

"If you say so," Carina said as she picked strands of shiny foil off his shirt and out of his hair.

Alexandra June Lazlo, Princess Sasha to her friends, celebrated her big day in style. The castle piñata swung from a low tree branch far enough away from the tables to give room for the treasures and candy soon to be released. "I can't thank you enough for the last-minute save," Emilia told Carina. "You should make these and sell them, too!"

The nine little girls wielded the stick and managed to dent Carina's creation, but it took Uncle Philip's help to free the candy and confetti. The fortress yielded its treasures spectacularly.

"Did you get pictures? Please tell me you took pictures," Carina said to Emmie as they watched the aftermath of a blindfolded Philip demolishing Carina's masterpiece with one strike. The shower of glittery confetti and candy landed mainly on him and the rush of five-year-old kids nearly knocked him over.

"Oh yes," Emmie said. "I certainly did. These are priceless." She scrolled through the dozens of photos she had taken. The look of terror on Philip's face as the kids headed toward him sent the ladies into rolls of laughter.

"I'm glad I added the confetti," Carina said, "and I'm sure Philip's glad the glitter was reserved for the outside."

Hearing his name, and sensing the reason for their laughter, Philip joined them and complained about their levity. "That was terrifying," he said. "First I wasn't sure I could break it, since Miss Whitley here is a master architect, and then the screams of delight sounded more like a war cry." The rest of the family sided with Emmie and Carina, requesting copies of the photos, and offering feigned admiration for Philip's bravery.

The kids were enjoying a game of tag while the grownups cleaned up the pinata remains. Glitter from the outside of the castle glistened on the lawn. Carina apologized to Emmie who assured her that it made the scene quite magical. "No worries. The glitter in the yard and on the kids caught the sunlight and the photos look awesome," Sassy's mom said. Lowering her voice, she added, "Philip is sparkling." She pointed to the picnic table where Philip was wiping his arms with a unicorn napkin, having given up on his hair. His best efforts had done little to rid his dark curls of the shining evidence.

Carina took pity on him and headed over to help. "You're covered in glitter, sir," she said as she pushed him onto the picnic bench. "I'm sorry."

"Are you?" he asked, letting her brush off his back.

"Not at all," she said. "It's a good look on you." He held his breath as she ran her fingers through his hair. "I think you have more in your hair than the kids do."

"Take you time," he said. "This is nice." He felt her pause. "Sorry for making you blush."

"How do you know I blushed?" Carina ruffled his hair.

"I didn't," he laughed.

She continued her work until they both decided it was a lost cause. When she tilted his chin up to brush pieces off his cheek, he grabbed her hand. "That's fine. I'm sure it'll all come off eventually."

"You look quite stunning, honestly," she said, reclaiming her hand. She brushed his cheek again.

He moved her hand away then tucked the long curl that draped over her shoulder back behind her ear. "You have glitter on your cheek, too," he said as he trailed his fingers along her jaw.

"Do I?" she asked.

"Maybe," he said and pulled her closer until their noses almost touched. "But with or without glitter, you my dear, are more than stunning."

"Philip!" Jay's call ended the interlude abruptly. "Grill's ready."

"Duty calls," he said and kissed her on the forehead. When he turned back halfway across the yard, she was still staring after him. He grinned and winked.

The rest of the afternoon passed quickly. Carina helped with clean up while Sasha opened presents. Philip found her in the kitchen.

"Hiding, Miss Whitley?" He stole a mini cupcake off the tray. She swatted his hand away as he reached for a second one.

"No," she said, "I'm guarding the desserts."

"How's that working out for you? Seems to me there are cupcakes disappearing," he said as he reached around her and snatched another.

"You are a child," she said as she handed him the tray to take into the dining room. "Make yourself useful."

"Yes ma'am," he said. His father was watching from the doorway behind Carina, and gave his son a secret fist-bump as he passed by.

An hour later, the party wrapped up. Philip and Carina prepared to leave. "Carina and I have an early day tomorrow," he explained. "The boss gave us the day off today to celebrate the successful opening, but we'll have a ton to do before the weekend."

While Carina said goodbye to the birthday girl, he pulled his parents and siblings aside. "So? What do you think?"

"I vote for a Christmas wedding," Cassandra said.

"Although I have a few weeks off in early August before classes start again. That'd be even better."

The rest of the family nodded in agreement. Philip grinned.

Chapter 19
You have perfect timing

The debrief on Tuesday with Mr. Mansfield lasted until almost noon. Their boss's excitement over the success of the opening meant few details made it to the discussion. Philip slipped Carina a note under the table. *We'll cover the important stuff over lunch, ok?*

Shortly after noon, Philip slid into a booth at the Mexican restaurant across campus. "I'm exhausted. How about you?" Philip asked. "We get to do this all over again in two weeks, too."

"Without your adorable family and the delicious catering, though," Carina said.

"They will be thrilled to be equated with the yummy food," he said. During the Easter weekend activities, Philip didn't hide his interest from her or his family. Even though her willingness to hold his hand could be attributed to the comfort amidst the craziness of his family, it was still a huge step. As much as he wanted to discuss their relationship, he knew they needed to stick to the post-grand opening debriefing. Carina was obviously more focused on their task.

"I've already added that company to our preferred vendor list, along with the security company, framing suppliers, and the interns." They both spread out their notes, and Carina opened her laptop to take notes. "We need to work on advertising and expanding the children's activities for the general opening. They're likely will be more families, don't you think?"

They talked through lunch and managed to make it through the entire list of feedback. "I'll get these typed up and sent to Mr. Mansfield. I agree that we don't need to include the kids' activity for now, since the rooms aren't completed and the number of children is uncertain. I've made a scavenger hunt that should keep the young ones, and their parents, engaged. We'll have prizes at the gift shop for all the participants. We'll have time after the first night to review any adjustments we need to make so you guys are all ready for the rest of the grand opening week. I'm sorry I won't be here to help, though," she said. The conference started Sunday night, and she was carpooling with a group from upstate, so she'd miss Sunday afternoon's events and rest of the first week of the public opening. "Will you be okay?"

"Me? Without you?" Philip asked. He paused until she looked up. "Never." He reached across the table and held out his hand. He was rewarded with a smile and her hand. "The museum? It will survive. Not well, but sufficiently."

"You're silly," she said. "I'm looking forward to the conference, but I will miss the museum," she said, "and you, of course."

"Of course," he said, tracing his finger along the inside of her wrist before he released her hand.

The baby was due in less than six weeks. Jay asked

Carina to babysit Sasha one night before the public opening. "I need to take my wife out, alone, before all our private time disappears," he said. "Do you think there's a night you could squeeze us in? I know you're busy with the opening, though, so we'll understand."

Since the donor gala, and conversations with Mira, Emilia, and her family, Carina realized she filled her schedule with constant activities as a defense mechanism. The healing of the past few weeks allowed her to objectively choose the most important ones. She had changed some weekly events to monthly, and the twin teenagers no longer needed her tutoring help since they were making consistently better grades now. The opening was a week away and she only had a few small tasks left to complete. Her Thursday evening was free.

"Hanging out with her would be a joy," Carina said. "It would help me, too. My ballet studio is considering a creative movement class for preschoolers and early elementary students. They want me to think about teaching it. I'd like to try some ideas out with Sassy."

The ballet studio's director attended a conference and returned with plans to expand their studio offerings to younger students. The lead teacher suggested Carina pull out some classic pop music, maybe even some oldies, have Sassy listen to the music, and just have fun. "The basics of any dance is listening to the music and learning to respond, first with no limits on your own expression, and then to build on that freeform to teach basic techniques," she had said. Carina was excited for the new opportunity. Dance classes started for her when she went to live with her aunt and uncle. It became the best therapy.

"Sounds like fun," Jay said. "We appreciate this so

much. Even though it's weeks away, Emmie's started to panic a bit about how much our lives are going to change with a newborn. I figure a night out is the least I can do."

Fancy grilled cheese sandwiches and tater tots for their dance party dinner won rave reviews from Miss Alexandra Lazlo. "Rina says I can put whatever I want on my sandwich," she told her parents as they prepared to leave. "I'm gonna have bacon and pickles and yellow cheese and holey cheese."

"Sounds delicious," her mom said. "Maybe I'll stay here instead of going out to a fancy restaurant and eating steak and lobster."

"Mommies and Daddies aren't invited to our dance party," Sassy said. "Rina said so."

Carina laughed and shooed the parents out the door. "Have fun, you two. Stay out as late as you want. We'll be fine."

The pair ate their gourmet creations and made cookies. While the overly sprinkled sugar cookies were baking, Carina pulled up the playlist she had created earlier. They pushed the coffee table and recliner out of the way so the living room became their dance floor. Twirling and jumping to selections from a favorite movie soundtrack lasted through the first batch of cookies. While those cooled, and the next baked, the dancing continued.

"Just listen to the song and the music, Sassy," she said. "You can even act out the words or jump and spin...whatever feels right."

The next song was one of Carina's favorites. Her mom had loved the Monkees and The Partridge Family, so 'I Think I Love You,' had played often in her childhood home and was an automatic choice for her playlist. She sang along and by the second chorus, Sassy joined in. They were giggling and serenading each other so they didn't hear their visitor arrive. As Carina was belting out, "*I think I love you,*" she spun toward the front door. Philip was leaning against the door jamb, grinning.

"Philip! What are you doing here?" Carina grabbed her phone and paused the song.

"Enjoying the performance of two beautiful dancers," he said as he picked up his young cousin, then reached for Carina's phone and turned the music back on.

His deep baritone voice blended with Sassy's giggles. Carina moved to a safe distance as he spun around, conveniently ending in front of her, meeting her gaze as he sang, repeating the title words as the song ended. "I love these lyrics," he said. "They convey so much, don't you think?"

The oven timer saved Carina from answering. "You have perfect timing," she said. Realizing the double meaning of her words before she could stop them, she avoided his gaze. "The second round of cookies are done. You timed your visit well."

"Yes," he said. "I did."

At the restaurant, Emilia Lazlo grinned as she read Philip's text. Her husband shook his head. "Did it work?" he asked. His wife nodded. Earlier that day, Philip had called to ask if he could borrow their crock pot.

"I didn't interfere, dearest," Emmie smiled at her husband. "He asked to come over. I told him we'd be out for dinner, but that since he has a key, he could come whenever."

"You conveniently left out a few details," Jay said, "including that your 'we' was only you and me, and that

Carina would be there with Sasha."

"Did I?" Emmie asked. "I must have had a pregnancy-induced fuzzy brain moment."

With the community grand opening now two days away, on Wednesday Carina maneuvered around the boxes that she was using to pack for the move to the new offices. The move replaced her other tasks on Mr. Mansfield's priority list. The office spaces on the second floor of the warehouse served as storage until last week. Now, with the spaces cleared and touch-up painting done, moving the furniture would be scheduled. When Carina returned from the conference, her office would be in the new building. Moving stressed her, but she'd learned to hide her anxiety. Knowing she'd be away at the conference helped, but she still didn't look forward to the process.

Philip saw her mood change and tried humor to bring back her smile, "I love what you've done with the place," he said. "Early American packing box period, correct?" When she didn't answer, he pulled her behind the stack of boxes, hiding them from view. "What's wrong, Carina?" He tilted her chin up. "Talk to me, please."

"I hate moving," she said. "That's all. It brings back memories I'd rather not dwell on. I'm glad I'll be gone for the official moving day."

Knowing there was history here but sensing now was not the time to press her, he pulled her into his arms. "I'm sorry. I'll personally make sure everything's organized for you. It looks like you've labeled the boxes well," he said. "Do you have to handle Mr. Mansfield's office, too?" He felt her nod and growled.

She giggled. "Listen Mr. Huntsman, you don't need to protect me from the Big Bad Wolf, which we both know is a big softie. Taking care of him is my job, sir. Plus, packing his office isn't stressful for some reason." She snuggled closer. Philip hoped she couldn't hear his pulse speed up. "And as fun as this is, I need to get back to it, sir."

He kissed her on the cheek and released her. "I'll be downtown all day tomorrow meeting with donors, and I hear Mr. Mansfield realized he'd be without his executive assistant for a week and he panicked, so your day is probably filled, right?"

"True. I'll be here until nine or later," she said.

"Can we talk about us before you leave for the conference?" He stopped in the doorway.

"Us? Me and you?" Her teasing tone earned a laugh as she leaned around the stack of boxes. "There's an 'us'?"

"Shall I explain with a demonstration?" Philip asked as he took a step back toward her.

"No need," She stopped him a raised hand. "I think that'd be a good idea. I don't leave until Sunday morning so I'll be at the first couple nights of the opening week. I'll be off on Saturday, but since the museum won't open that day until noon, how about breakfast, around eight? I'll cook."

"Perfect. Saturday it is."

"Until then, try not to miss me too terribly," she said, grinning widely.

"Impossible," he said. He clung to the picture of that smile for days.

The craziness of Friday at the museum meant she and Philip only saw each other a couple of times as they dealt with issues typical of a new museum opening. Spotting him across the modern art wing, she waved and sent him a text. *Too bad we don't have the catered buffet filled with sweets tonight.* He smiled and responded.

I'm starving! Hopefully, you're prepared to feed a hungry bear tomorrow morning.

She typed her response without looking his way, *Of course. A full meal including scrambled eggs and orange juice.* She turned away and returned to the children's activity room, but not before she heard his laughter.

Splendid. I can't wait.

Mr. Mansfield sought her out before closing and encouraged her to head home. "I know you're leaving early on Sunday and you probably have a list of last-minute projects to handle tomorrow. Keep us posted on the conference, and I look forward to all the new ideas you bring home." Carina looked through several galleries with no success in locating Philip, so she asked Tess to let him know she was leaving. By early evening she was prepping the food for their breakfast date, when a knock at her door changed everything.

A delivery arrived that shook Carina's carefully reconstructed fortress. As she signed for the packages, she noted the return address. It was an unfamiliar street, but the same city where she had spent those fateful weeks so many years ago. The packages had to be from the Booths. Carina called her aunt and uncle.

"I think I know what's in the big box—the chest

with our family photo albums. I know the memories will be overwhelming so I'm not sure if I'll open it now or not. I have the entire day to recover, so I may chance it."

"What about the envelope? Do you have any idea what's in it?" her uncle asked.

"No idea. I don't want to open it and face whatever's in it since it's probably from Mrs. Booth or her daughter, but I'm afraid if I don't open it I'll be robbing myself of something important."

Her aunt and uncle suggested that she wait until after the conference to decide about opening it. "Maybe you should have someone with you when you do. Philip would be willing, wouldn't he?"

Carina had been open with her family about Philip. He met them over video chat when they realized they wouldn't be at the ballet and she'd called them several times when Philip was with her. They knew about the encounter with Mrs. Booth's daughter, and Philip's role in helping her find closure.

"He may not be ready for that," she said.

"Will you be able to take some time after the conference for a short break as you'd hoped?" Aunt Lynette asked, not pressing her niece for an explanation of her hesitancy. "You've chosen busyness for so long to avoid facing a lot of these memories. Maybe this opportunity away is God's timing for you."

Carina agreed and promised to confirm with Mr. Mansfield. "Thank you both for the encouragement and prayer."

"We'll see you in May," her aunt. "Get some rest and wait as long as you need to before opening either package or envelope. We love you."

Carin called Mr. Mansfield, confirmed the additional days off, then stared at the chest she'd unpacked from the large box. As she lifted the lid, she broke down as the memories flooded in. Thumbing through the oldest photo album brought back bittersweet memories that she'd locked away for years. Thinking about how to hide her puffy eyes from her fellow passengers in the morning, she decided to wait to unpack any more. "I'll face you when I get back," she said as she closed the chest. She picked up the envelope several times, moving it from the coffee table to the kitchen counter, and back. Finally, she stuffed it into her large duffel bag. She could stare at it just as well at the conference.

Saturday came. Carina looked again at Philip's last text. *Splendid. I can't wait,* he had written.

Today was anything but perfect. The memories haunted her all night and she was in no shape to for what might have been a romantic, fun meal. She texted him a few minutes before seven that morning. He was at the gym, getting a workout in before their breakfast.

I'm sorry, something's come up. Please don't call or come by to check on me. I'll be fine. We'll talk when I get back.

Philip ignored her request and called before he left the gym, but only reached her voicemail. After a quick shower he stood in the hallway staring at her apartment door. It was eight o'clock. He called again, with no better result. He slumped back into his apartment, slamming the door in an act of childishness. He'd have to apologize to his neighbors later. Although she had Saturday off, he did not, and an issue with one of the displays called him back to duty. It was several hours before he called again. Frustrated, he considered filling her voicemail with messages, but he sent a text instead.

Are you okay? Call me, please.

As she folded her last load of laundry, Carina read Philip's text but didn't respond. She'd spent the rest of the day cleaning her apartment, packing, and ignoring his calls.

Sunday morning she composed a couple texts, wrote a note for the likely visitor to her apartment, and headed for the lobby. Her ride had texted and was running late. She almost dropped her bag when she saw that Philip was waiting for her as she exited the elevator.

"Philip! Why aren't you at church?" she asked. The museum events started mid-afternoon, so she thought he would be able to make it to the early service.

He grabbed her bags and put them by the door. "I wanted to see you off," he said, reaching for her hand. She let him hold it, but couldn't stop thinking about the unopened box. He saw the signs left from last night's tears and frowned. "Are you okay?"

She mentally shook away the fog and forced a smile. "Yes, just tired," she lied. "I figured it'd be rude to sleep the entire trip so I've had two cups of strong coffee already this morning."

He handed her the bakery bag he'd left on the kiosk. "Here's a croissant to tide you over until lunch. I'm sure you didn't eat with your mega dose of coffee, am I right?"

"Yes, you are," she said. "Thank you. I'm looking forward to the conference, and honestly I think the time apart will be good for me."

His frown needed no explanation. He disagreed, but didn't want to distress her. "If you think so, Carina."

Her ride arrived before she could respond. He put her bags in the car before pulling her into a quick hug. 'I'll try to be patient. Please don't wait too long, though."

Chapter 20
Maybe that's all it was

"Does bad news come in threes?" Philip asked Emilia Monday afternoon. "Because if it does, look out. Something terrible is about to happen." That morning Mr. Mansfield informed him Carina would be gone at least a week.

"I'm sure Miss Whitley contacted you already. I planned to offer her some bonus time off anyway, after my wife explained, and the reviews from the opening confirmed, that Miss Whitley's role in our success was paramount. When she called late Friday night and explained that a family matter had arisen, I was glad to be able to extend her time away after the conference," her boss said. "She informed the new Mrs. Stafford of the matters that can be handled without her and also left you a list with her apologies."

Philip pulled out his latent acting skills and didn't reveal his shock or disappointment. "We'll handle it all, sir. Tess will be prepared. Don't worry." When Carina didn't answer his text, he hoped it was because she was on the road. Since she was carpooling and probably not driving, he thought she might answer. Several texts and phone calls later, worry set in. All he could think of was her last words. *Why had she said, 'time apart,' and not 'time away,'* he thought.

Emilia offered no insight. The only communication she'd had with Carina was the cryptic text she received after Carina was on the road. *Tell Philip I'm sorry. Try to convince him not to worry or panic.* It was no more help than her note to him. *I'm sorry. I need a few days before we can talk. Please keep praying for me and try not to worry.*

"Try not to worry? What am I? Superhuman? Vulcan?" Philip called his aunt on the way out of Mr. Mansfield's office and again when he got home. "I'm going to check her apartment for clues." There was a note on the counter. Carina knew he'd end up there.

"I'm fine. Don't panic. Saturday's breakfast is in the fridge. It'll heat up easily in the microwave. After all that's happened recently, I hope you'll understand my change in plans. I need some time alone to make sure I'm in a good place, with my priorities clear, before we can make any 'us' decisions."

Glancing at his watch, Philip guessed Carina would be at the conference center by now, possibly at dinner. He decided to try one more time. Offering a simple prayer that this wouldn't create a bigger rift, he worded his text carefully. *I know we may be moving faster than is wise. You're dealing with the shock from the ballet event. I will slow down. I will miss you and hope you have a great conference.*

Carina ignored his texts until she settled into her room. The first evening session didn't start for an hour. The six-hour ride to Panama City conference center gave her time to think. Too much time. Philip's parting message repeated in her mind. *'Don't wait too long.'*

"What does that mean?" she said as she stared at her reflection in the hotel mirror. Looking at her phone for the hundredth time, Philip's numerous texts and missed calls seem to yell at her. Knowing her text app let her see the messages without letting the sender know they'd been received, she read them. She could hear his voice. *'Why didn't you tell me? What happened?'* followed by *'Are you okay? Call me, please..,'* and similar statements filled the texts. His last text cemented her confusion.

"He thinks we're moving too fast," she said to her aunt when she called to let her know she'd arrived safely. "I finally admitted my interest in 'us' and now he wants to slow down."

"You did ask for time, my dear," Aunt Lynette reminded her.

"I know, I know," Carina said. "Your suggestion that I take some time away is sounding increasingly sensible. I have the freedom to stay for a few days. I told the boss that I'd be gone until next week."

"What did Philip say when you told him?"

"I didn't tell him," Carina said.

"Ah," her aunt said, "Then don't read more into those texts than is actually there. It sounds to me like he was panicking, not pushing away. We'll be praying for you. Try to concentrate on having a good time at the conference," she added, knowing her niece well, "and relax!"

Before she fell asleep, Carina checked her phone once more. Her hand hesitated as she opened the voicemail. She closed it without listening. Hearing his voice was a step too far.

On the other end of that call, her aunt faced a dilemma. "I should have told her," Lynette Whitley said.

A few days after Carina received the envelope and chest, a letter arrived at their house from Mrs. Booth's daughter. The neighbor picked up their mail and had called to see if it was important enough to forward to them. Recognizing the return address she read to them, they asked her to open it.

Clara Danvers had written, '*I hope I haven't over-stepped, but after observing Mr. Corelli's attention to Carina, I let my romantic notions lead my actions. I'm sending her mother's wedding and engagement rings to you. If I've erred in any way, please send them on to Carina with my apologies. The depth of my regret for all that happened during those awful weeks didn't deserve the forgiveness and gentleness she expressed to me and my mother. Thank you for being a supportive, godly family.*'

"What should we do now?" Carina's aunt asked her husband. "I don't know if Carina's ever questioned where her parents' personal articles went after the accident. She was so young. Now she may have assumed these were lost, or may think they're in the chest. I know she hasn't had time to go through it."

"I say punt to Philip," her husband said. "I can text him and tell him about the ring." At his wife's look of dismay, he laughed. "Don't they say it's easier to ask for forgiveness than permission?"

"You're so funny, my dear," she said, "and oh so helpful."

The conference seminars supplied Carina so many ideas that she purchased a second notebook to record them. Vendors samples filled another bag. Carina figured paying for a second suitcase if she flew back home would be a good idea.

Her appointment with two seasoned children and family activity coordinators encouraged her. They loved her vision for reaching the underserved communities and suggested she reach out to the schools in the area during the summer. Most schools had staff on site during the break and could point her toward the teachers and administrators that would be the most help.

Tess received daily texts and photos from Carina with ideas for new products to purchase for the gift shop. "I'll get you as many samples as I can," she said when she called halfway through the conference.

"Philip asked about the conference yesterday," Tess said. "He was here finishing the preparations for Monday's opening. You'll be missed."

"He said that?" Carina said.

"No, but I know he wanted to," Tess laughed. "You two aren't fooling anyone, you know."

Carina cringed. "I'm not sure it's as serious as you think it is," she said. "His engagement ended so recently, plus I certainly haven't been looking for a real relationship." Of course, their recent interactions played in her head. She knew where her feelings were heading, but her interpretation of his interest bounced between being simple flirtation to something more serious. Not voicing these thoughts, she simply added, "We spent so much time working on the museum opening together and we're friends, but I think that maybe that's all it was."

"Whatever you say," Tess said, holding back her skepticism. "He seemed distraught in case you want to know. I'm sure it's tough handling the opening without you here."

"He'll be fine, and he has you to help," Carina said. "The next meeting is starting. I need to scoot since tomorrow's the last day. I don't want to miss any sessions." Carina hoped her tone covered her real feelings. The text from Philip saying that they should 'slow down' played repeatedly in her mind. The unopened envelope in her hotel room only added to her fears. Would her past always overshadow her future? Did knowing change the outlook for her and Philip in his eyes? She could hear romantic but suspenseful music playing behind her thoughts like a bad soap opera. "You're being ridiculous, Carina," she said to her reflection in the hotel mirror.

She knew she needed time to think, so she decided to take her aunt's advice. Mr. Mansfield had given her the days off, but taking the break away from home would be more helpful than moping around her apartment.

The bonus the museum board gave the staff covered the cost of a few extra days at the beach. Her uncle recommended a hotel further out from Panama City beach, away from the crowds. It was owned by a friend of his, and despite being smaller, offered luxury accommodations and a shuttle to the airport. Carina planned to fly home or rent a car. It was a decision she'd make later.

It was the last day of the conference. Risking crossing the lines she'd laid out for her time away, she called Emilia. "Just to check on the baby," she said. "I know you're heading into the third trimester. Are you getting enough rest?"

Emilia ignored the question and jumped to peppering Carina with questions, "What's going on with you and my nephew? He's driving us crazy. Where are you? What happened?"

Carina could only laugh, before filling in the details for her friend. "I received a couple packages before I left. One is a mystery but I'm sure it's from Mrs. Booth or her daughter, Carla. I haven't opened it yet," she said, explaining her apprehension, but not revealing that the other package had been what caused the tears Philip had suspected. "Please don't tell Philip. I think he thinks whatever is happening between us is moving too fast, and maybe he's even changed his mind."

Emmie's laughter confused her.

"Am I missing something?" Carina asked. Realizing she may have misinterpreted his texts, and thinking back to her messages, she knew her words were vague enough to cause confusion, also. "I'm not sure he understood my messages."

Emmie realized Carina was serious, so she switched to 'big sister, caring aunt, interfering friend' mode. She assured Carina that Philip's feelings were as strong as ever. "He's playing Sherlock Holmes, trying to find you. He's hooked, for sure." The limits of a phone call meant Emmie didn't see Carina's reaction. "Don't tell me where you are—I wouldn't be able to keep it a secret," Emmie said, "plus I think he's having a good time playing detective. It'll do him good to suffer a little."

"I promised myself not to respond to his texts or calls, and I know it's best for me to stick to that," Carina said, still processing Emmie's words and reactions. "Have I made a huge mistake?"

Emilia heard the concern in Carina's voice. Choosing bluntness, she asked, "Are you in love with my nephew?"

Chapter 21
What took you so long?

Social media complicates many lives, but for Philip's quest to find Carina, it was a godsend. On Monday morning, Tess had shown him some of the photos Carina sent of ideas for new inventory in the gift shop. She let him scroll through while she waited on a customer. One of the last photos was of a picture in the lobby of her hotel. The photo's date indicated it'd been taken after the conference had ended. Philip spent the evening searching through websites of hotels. It took a couple of hours, and twenty-something websites, before he located the hotel lobby that matched the photo.

"Gotcha!" he said.

"Got who?" Tess asked, looking over his shoulder. "Oh! You found her. Please don't tell her that you got any information from me, although I don't think she'll be surprised."

Jay and Emilia's lengthy discussion ended in a standstill. "He needs to know," Emmie had said.

"Leave the two of them alone," Jay said. "It'll work itself out." When his wife's cute pout appeared he caved in. "Let's compromise. You can tell him to not abandon his search. Remind him that she told him not to panic."

He kissed his wife, and added, "I think he's suffered enough."

Suffer, he had. "Six days have felt like six years," Philip told Jay. "I think I found her, though. Now I need to decide when—or if—I'm going to go after her."

"Looks like the competition has been good for you, even if it was just a competition with Carina's doubts." Jay grinned. "The conference ended Tuesday, right? Do you want to fly or drive? I'll book your rental," he said, pulling out his phone. "What time do you want to leave?"

It was Thursday morning. Philip knew he had enough time to get to Carina by mid-afternoon. Mr. Mansfield, a well-known romantic, gave Philip the days off he needed. "The opening went smoothly, and I trust the staff to handle any issues. Tell Miss Whitley we have missed her."

First, though, he needed to make a call. Since he met Carina's family on their video call weeks ago, he had talked to them numerous times, both with and without Carina. "We promised not to reveal her location, Philip," her uncle said, "but we're thrilled that you're not giving up on your relationship. We've been praying for you both."

"I appreciate that," Philip said. "Carina's trust means more to me than I can say. I'm hoping she'll see how much I care for her, and how much I hope we have a future together. Do you think I'm moving too fast? Any advice you can give, I'd appreciate." Philip knew his nervousness was making him ramble.

The Whitley's encouraged him and teased him a bit. "You're perfect for Carina, Philip. She talks about you all the time, and although we understand why she needed some time alone this week, don't be discouraged," Aunt Lynette said. "You have our full support. Go, find her, but be patient. She needs you right now and I think she'll be willing to admit that."

"If you're flying down," Clark Whitley said, "you might want to get a one-way ticket. From my experience, a five- or six-hour car ride is a great conversation opportunity."

Ten minutes later, Philip booked his flight and reserved a rental car. Jay contacted the hotel and secured a room for the night. Philip landed in Florida three hours later.

The evening sunset over the Gulf of Mexico rarely disappointed. Carina lowered her book to enjoy the view. Tonight she had the deck to herself. The other hotel guests, not many in number, were either at dinner or out enjoying the evening elsewhere. She smiled at the children chasing the waves on the beach below. *Peacefulness, rest, clarity. This is what I needed.* The time away had been helpful and tomorrow she'd be heading back home, more hopeful and content than when she left. As the sun sank closer to the horizon, she picked up her book, planning to finish the current chapter before the light faded. The sound of the hotel door stopped her.

"This way, sir," she heard Ronaldo, the hotel caretaker's son. As the newcomer approached, she kept her eyes on the book.

"Hello, Philip," she said, calmly turning the pages. "What took you so long?"

"What took me so long?" He freed the book from her hands and sat on the end of the chaise lounge. "You have some nerve asking me that, ma'am." He lifted her foot.

"Sandals or no sandals?"

She started to pull her foot away but he refused to release it. "Am I scaring you?"

"Yes," and "no," responses came in unison. Philip grinned. Carina rescued the young man still standing behind her chair.

"Ronaldo, I was expecting Mr. Corelli. He's not going to hurt me. Forgive us for frightening you," she said. "Thank you for delivering him safely. Can you please take my bag inside? I'll get it later." The young man took the bag and escaped.

"We'll be walking on the beach," Philip explained. Holding up the sandals he'd just removed, he addressed Carina once more. "I'm guessing you'll be fine without these?" He stowed them along with his under the chair, then held out his hand. "Let's go."

Philip relaxed as Carina complied. She pulled him to a stop at the bottom of the stairs leading to the beach. "Philip, stop for a minute," she said.

He turned to face her and released her hand. She smiled and slipped her arms around his waist. "Thank you for finding me," she said, resting her head on his chest. "I'm sorry I didn't tell you everything before I left for the conference."

"Let's walk," he said. "You can apologize more completely." She poked him in the ribs as they stepped onto the sand. Philip laced his fingers with hers. They walked for several minutes without talking. Finally Carina broke the silence.

"How did you find me? Let me guess," she said. "It was Emmie or Tess, or maybe Sassy?"

"I refuse to reveal my sources," he said. "Perhaps I'm simply a great detective."

"Sure, you are," she said. "I'll hire you when I start my spy agency."

They paused their walk to watch the sun sink behind the horizon. Philip pulled her in front of him and rested his chin on her head as they watched the sunset. "That's beautiful," Carina said. "I've always loved sunsets, but sunrises are my favorite. They always remind me of new beginnings."

"Carina, what happened before the conference? Did it have something to do with the chest I saw on your coffee table?" He turned her to face her. "I didn't open it, but you left this on the kitchen counter." He pulled an old photo from his pocket. It was a Christmas picture of a mom and dad and little girl. "Is this you?" He brushed away the stray tear. "You were adorable," he said, "and still are."

They continued down the beach, giving her a chance to recover. She explained that the chest was the one she thought had been lost. "I wasn't ready for the emotions that hit me, so I only pulled out a few photos before I had to stop. I don't know when I'll be able to finish going through it."

"I'll be there to help you, if you want," Philip said.

"Thank you," she said, "but that wasn't all. There was a large envelope delivered, too. I didn't open it. I brought it with me and have been staring at it all week. I have no idea what could be in it, and I'm not sure I want to know."

Philip stopped and pulled her into his arms. "I'm so sorry, Carina. If I could take the pain away I would. I'm here for you to vent, yell at, or just sit with."

"This right here is nice," she said, squeezing him gently. "You smell good."

Philip laughed. "My aftershave company will appreciate your endorsement." He traced a slow line along her cheek. "I can picture the commercial now. A young couple walking along a deserted beach, a beautiful sunset, soft music in the background. They stop. He pulls her into a romantic embrace and she gazes into his eyes. With a sigh, she says, 'You smell good.' It'll be award-winning."

"I've missed your silliness," she said.

They spotted an ice cream shop along the boardwalk. "How on earth can you eat that?" Carina asked as Philip started to bubblegum ice cream. "You're a child."

"You're not a fan? I'll get something else, in case we decide to share," he said, wiggling his eyebrows suggestively.

"I'm not sharing, buddy." Carina pretended to miss the implication. "Tell me about the rest of the opening events," she said as the server presented their cones. "Any hiccups?"

The community opening's success surprised Mr. Mansfield, but not Philip and the rest of the staff. Carina's handling of the donor and investor's opening made this one easier. "Your idea of the scavenger hunt for the children was brilliant," Philip said. "It kept the kids occupied as much as the art did for the original event. When we get all the classrooms completed, I'm pushing for one to be turned into an art activity center. The success of the children's activity at the first opening shows that there's an interest for this."

It was dark by the time they started back, but the lights from the boardwalk offered soft light to the beach. They walked through the edge of the surf.

"This is romantic," Carina said. "I'm glad you came

for me and having you know my story is comforting." She slowed their pace and finally stopped. "I sense, though, that there's something you need to say."

Philip pulled her close once more. "Honestly, we both know what's going on here, and I'm admitting now that it was going on a lot longer than you probably realize. I hesitated to tell you how I felt because I didn't want to scare you, plus there was that other situation I had to take care of."

"True," Carina said, slipping her arms around his neck. "But before we delve too far into this deep discussion, I have a request."

"Anything," Philip said.

"Could you kiss me, please?" Carina tilted her chin up. "Unless you don't want to," she said.

"Ah, how I've missed your humor, my dear," he said. "Kissing you is something I've wanted to do for many, many weeks.."

On the ride home, Carina filled in some of the questions she knew Philip hadn't asked.

"Philip, you can ask me about what happened to me, and I'll answer what I can. Many years of therapy have helped me accept that my reactions as a six-year-old were normal. As I got older, I felt guilt at one point, since my abuse was mild compared to what others experienced." She raised a hand to stop him, seeing his objection coming.

"Yes, Mira explained that there's no 'benign' abuse. Mrs. Booth's son only physically hurt me once, pushing me out of the way when I tried to protect her the first day I was with them. That, added to the more difficult trauma of losing my parents, is why the delivery of the chest sent me into this spiral. I know you understand why I don't remember all the details, though."

"May I ask why your aunt and uncle weren't contacted sooner?" Philip asked. "I realize they were probably overseas, but…"

"It's okay, Philip," Carina said. "There's an explanation. My uncle worked for the government at the time and well, there were 'security' protocols that delayed the news in the first place. Then they had difficulty getting out of the country they were in at the time for a variety of reasons."

"Sounds like a spy novel," Philip said.

"You didn't hear that from me," Carina said. The light-hearted break from her story was welcome, but short.

For several days after the accident, Carina didn't speak. When she was placed with Mrs. Booth, the church family kept in touch, but had an extended vacation planned soon after they helped clear out and sell the house. The isolation compounded the emotional scars Carina experienced.

"They cut their trip short when the news of my situation reached them. I stayed with them for a couple weeks before my aunt and uncle arrived." Child services agreed to let her stay with the church family until the next of kin could be located. Their care for the shock-stricken little girl, both before and after her stay with the Booths, was vital.

Carina smiled and patted Philip's arm when she saw his tight grip on the steering wheel.

"Philip, I know you can't imagine how I got through the pain, and honestly sometimes it does wash over me again," she said. "But I know my Heavenly Father is stronger than anything bad that happened or can happen to me." When he only nodded, she added, "Being able to share my story with you has given me a healing I didn't know I was missing." Still unable to talk, Philip simply lifted her hand to his lips.

Humor once again intervened. She teased him about his expert driving, despite her obvious ability to distract him. "It's one of my newly acquired talents," he said. "Started in January of this year, if I recall correctly."

"When you're ready to open that envelope, I'll be there if you want," Philip said as he carried her luggage to her apartment.

"I think I'll wait until my aunt and uncle come," she said. "I'm sure we'll be going through the photo albums. I know you offered already, but I'd love for you to join us."

Chapter 22
I'll question your logic later

As Lynette and Clark Whitley continued their foreign travel, they still made it back to the States every year at Mother's Day, and were able some years to stay through Father's Day. This year the visit would only last a week, but their July reunion plans were in place and they had additional news for Carina.

"I'm finally retiring from travel, Carina," Clark told her. "I have to make one more trip after we leave here, but after that we'll be settling back near the home office in Jacksonville. We'll be here for the reunion and should be settled in our new home by the end of summer. Since we won't be far away, you'll probably get tired of seeing us."

"Impossible," Carina said. "I know I shouldn't have to repeat myself, but you two are welcome to stay in my apartment. The couch is comfortable. I know from experience." Her uncle frowned, knowing the story behind her words. Carina changed the subject.

"I have half a day off on Friday so we can hit some of the area sites. I'm sorry I couldn't take more time off, but the week I was gone for the conference put me behind on preparations for the children's programs." Her family knew the importance of the children's programs that would begin in a couple of weeks, in time for the public schools' summer break.

"We've been invited to the Lazlos for dinner on Saturday, but if you're tired they will understand," she continued, thinking how to explain the disappointment to Sassy…and Philip.

"It's already on our list," Clark said and endured the 'look' from his wife. Philip alerted them to the invitation several days ago. Carina's uncle backpedaled. "You told us about it already, remember?"

She wasn't fooled, but let it go. All parties involved looked forward to meeting in person at last and several had deeper motives. Carina's aunt and uncle hoped to get a clearer picture of the relationship between their niece and Philip. Their worries proved unnecessary. The families blended instantly.

Clark regaled Alexandra with tales of her namesake, Alexander the Great—and his father Philip. He showed her pictures on his phone of landmarks including the statue of Sofia the goddess of wisdom in Bulgaria, castles in Spain and Germany, and the Eiffel Tower. The kindergartener caught the travel bug quickly.

"I want to grow up and travel to 'your rope,' too," she said. Clark laughed, but didn't correct the girl's wording.

"Maybe we can take you someday. That would be fun," he said, not yet familiar with her 'Sassy' and spontaneous personality.

"Mommy! Uncle Clark and Aunt Lynette are going to take me to see castles and pointy towers and pretty statues! Do you wanna come, too?" Philip and Carina rescued Clark and took Sasha for a walk, "to work off the delicious dinner and the extra energy."

Jay mumbled to his wife, "So that's what they're calling it these days?" Clark overheard and laughed.

"My thoughts exactly," he said to a red-faced Jay. "At least they have a chaperone."

While cleaning up the dinner table, the four adults discussed Philip and Carina. The conversation proved insightful and fruitful. All agreed to do everything they could to encourage the couple.

So many details of her past remained unshared, but Philip stayed patient. When Carina told him her family wouldn't be at church, he had trusted their reasons. It was Mother's Day and that alone gave reason enough to want time away from any celebrations. 'Skipping' church on Mother's Day started the first year after the accident. Her wise aunt and uncle knew that all the looks of condolence and compassion would compound her pain, especially with the pain of what she'd experienced in their absence. The tradition continued even though Carina now took both Mother's Day and Father's Day to celebrate the memories of her time with her parents and the people she knew them to be through conversations with their friends and relatives over the years.

Today, the trio strolled through a park near the college after their traditional pancake breakfast on Mother's Day. Carina's annual reflections seemed less despondent this year and both her aunt and uncle noticed. As they walked, they shared more from their recent trip, reminisced about her parents, and described the 'dream house' they hoped to build soon near the Florida coast. Then their conversation turned to Philip.

"We like him, Carina," her aunt said. "Have you told him yet?"

Not bothering to pretend she didn't know what her aunt meant, Carina shook her head. "Not yet. I've come close, as has he, I think. He did introduce me as his girlfriend recently." She smiled as she remembered their second meeting with Mei at her parents' restaurant. The precocious little girl had given Philip a thumbs up which he had to explain to Carina later.

"We know it's tricky when you work with someone you're interested in," Clark said, giving his wife of forty years a swift kiss. "Both you and Philip need to be honest with each other, and your boss. But if what we observed is any indication, everyone at work already knows."

Monday night Philip joined them as they went through the photo albums from the chest. Carina had been through them several times already, so she was able to enjoy the memories without the sadness. Lynette and Clark provided Philip with background on many of the photos that Carina was too young to remember. They took a break when the dinner arrived. American style pizza was a treat the Whitleys never outgrew.

When they finished, Carina put a batch of brownies in the oven, and the topic of the envelope arose.

"Are you ready to open this, dearest?" Clark placed the legal-sized package on the counter.

"Yes," Carina said. "I've prepared myself for the worst and am hoping for the best." She and Philip had speculated on their trip home from Florida. Thinking it could be details of her ordeal, possibly even the police reports, photos, or transcripts, frightened her. Philip suggested it might hold financial news or personal correspondence. Thankfully, his guess was closer than hers.

The envelope held several sealed envelopes, some postmarked weeks after her parents' passing. A handwritten note from Carla Danvers explained that the correspondence enclosed arrived at her mother's home after Carina had been removed. It had been forwarded so the lateness of delivery wasn't surprising. Her mom put it out of sight of her stepson and when Carina was taken by protective services her access to Carina was cut off.

Her parents' will contained no surprises since the county probate office had the official filing that was given to her uncle years ago. A letter from her parents that they had written at a couples retreat when she was a toddler, listing their hopes, dreams, and prayers for her brought the entire group to tears.

"We should've left that one until last," Philip said. "I need a brownie." The timer rang as the words left his mouth, sending them into peals of laughter.

The remaining envelopes brought welcome and unexpected news. A life insurance policy and a safe deposit box key, the latter with an explanation, promising treasures passed to Carina's mom from her maternal grandparents.

"Wow," Uncle Clark said. "This is fantastic. God is good. We all know that, but it's humbling at times to see it in such a concrete way."

"We're going to leave you two alone. This has been emotional for all of us and I know we all need time to process it."

Philip had gathered Carina into his arms and simply nodded to her family.

"Is that okay with you, Carina?" Her aunt knelt beside her and kissed her gently. "We can stay if you want."

"No," Carina raised her head. "We're good here. Take my car and swing by and get me for breakfast in the morning."

Philip walked the couple to their car, at Clark's request. He confessed the subterfuge about the ring, handing the small box to Philip. "I don't think she'll be angry, but if she is, make sure you let her know it was all our choice," Clark told him. "She's mentioned the rings and we've left our answer vague, telling her we're sure they'll be found sometime. We have boxes still in storage, so although it's a stretch of the truth, she seemed to be satisfied."

"So my question about your approval wouldn't be a surprise?"

"No, on the contrary," Clark said. "We'd be disappointed if you didn't ask." He offered his hand. "Tonight has confirmed all our first impressions. You have our full support. We are looking forward to welcoming you to the family."

The next Friday morning found Carina in a dangerous position. She had purchased magnetic moveable frames to put on the wall in the children's classroom. When she saw these frames in one of Philip's gallery catalogs, she knew immediately she wanted them for the children's space. Research and reviews affirmed their quality. One children's museum owner said they were 'game changers,' making changing displays easy and affordable.

The hall outside the classrooms featured art pieces catered to younger audiences. Carina framed those with repurposed leftover pieces donated by the company that framed the major artworks for the museum. She wanted the classroom to feature artwork made by children in the program classes. Advertisements and registration forms for the children's classes had been available since the community opening, and there were already several dozen signed up. A busy summer schedule made Carina thankful the board had scheduled the donor gala and the community grand opening before the college's graduation so the kinks worked themselves out before the increased crowds that weekend overwhelmed them. The whole staff gained encouragement and pushed for the children's programs to be ready on time.

Anxious to get the frames mounted and filled, Carina didn't wait for help. She climbed on a chair, but not one of the new upholstered, well-padded chairs sitting still in their boxes in the hallway. No, this was a rickety metal chair Carina found left over by one of Jasper's crew.

Carina hated heights. Even standing on a chair two feet off the ground made her nervous, but she needed to get these frames placed. The double frames held the artwork between them and hung on magnetic circles attached to the wall with poster putty. They would allow the children's artwork to be displayed and changed out easily.

Warming the putty in her hands meant she had to lean against the wall to keep her balance. When she reached to place the first circle, the chair swayed. "This was not a good idea, ma'am," she said aloud.

"What are you doing?" The voice from the door startled Carina enough to make a fall inevitable. Or it would've been inevitable had Philip not reached her in time. He grabbed her waist and steadied her. As she rested against him, he waited until she caught her breath, and until his heart stopped pounding. "I'm going to help you down."

"No, I'm okay," she said as she straightened up. "I need to finish this."

"I'm not letting go until you are on the floor," Philip said. "So it's your choice, Miss 'I'm Afraid of Heights.' Either get down now, or do what you need while I hold you up."

"Fine," she said. "Just don't tickle me."

Philip resisted the temptation she presented and simply enjoyed the closeness. "Tell me what you're doing," he said. "I'll question your logic later."

Carina explained as she attached the other three circles. Philip listened half-heartedly as she stretched to reach the far corner. When she finished attaching the last circle, he relaxed enough to be impressed, until she wanted him to let go and hand her the frame that was on the table. They argued until she stomped her foot and almost took both of them over.

"Okay, okay," he said. "You win, but do not move." He grabbed the frame and handed it to her as he slipped his arm around her waist, securing her more than before. "This is ridiculous, you know. If you'd just let me do this everyone would be happier."

"Says you," Carina said as she placed the frame on the

circles. "Back up and tell me if this is straight."

"It's straight," he said without moving. "Are you done? I no longer believe that you're afraid of heights, miss."

She wiggled around to face him, her chin level with his nose. He leaned back to see her better. "I still don't like heights," she said, "but this doesn't seem to bother me."

"It doesn't?" He caught his breath as she ran her hands across his shoulders and rested her forehead against his.

"No. I'm enjoying this," she said.

"Carina." Philip's low growl didn't prove warning enough as she slipped her arms around his neck. "You may be enjoying this but that doesn't mean this isn't dangerous. What are you doing?"

She giggled and moved her hands back to his shoulders. "Sorry. I think I was so relieved not to have fallen that I'm a little giddy," she said. "I don't ever feel frightened when you're around. It's strange. You can put me down now."

He lifted her off the chair but didn't release her. "I'll ask for an explanation later about why you decided to act so foolishly," he said, "but now, I'm going to tell you something and then ask you a question."

"Certainly," she said. Her hands paused from smoothing his lapels. "Anything you need. I'm here for you."

This was not what Philip had pictured for this moment. No romantic moonlight, no soft music, but as he stared at Carina he knew it was perfect.

"I love you Carina Whitley," he said. "I have for a

very long time and I'm sorry I haven't told you before." A sigh, smile, and her head on his shoulder were her only response for several moments.

"I love you too, Philip Corelli," she said, moving her head slightly. Her breath was warm against his neck. "I should have also told you sooner so there's no need to apologize." She leaned back and placed both hands on his cheeks. "As far as the romance of the moment, this is beautiful. Honestly," she said. "You said there was a question?"

"Despite our agreement to temper our affections in the workplace, I'd like to kiss you, Miss Whitley," Philip said. "Would that be acceptable?"

Carina's wide smile answered his question. The soft kiss lasted only a moment, interrupted by the sound of the museum's outer door. Philip growled and Carina laughed.

"We'll finish this *discussion* later," he said as he ran a finger down her cheek and released her. "I'll finish these frames for you."

She had marked the placement on the wall with faint pencil marks, making it easy for the two of them to finish in a few minutes. As she put away the supplies, she asked, "Were you looking for me when you got here?" She turned after closing the boxes. "Or was that a fortuitous coincidence? Although if you hadn't yelled at me I wouldn't have almost fallen and your rescue would have been unnecessary."

"Yes, Mr. Mansfield wants to meet with us, and no ma'am, I will not take responsibility for your high wire act," he said. "I think we used the time well, though, don't you?"

She rewarded him with another kiss. As Philip returned the dangerous chair to its place, he added, "But I will not apologize for rescuing you. Ever."

The frantic pace of the pre-opening weeks settled into more manageable hours, for Philip more than Carina who was busy with the children's programs. Since the public school's summer break started, her days involved juggling the art education interns and still fulfilling her Executive Assistant duties.

Over the course of a couple of weeks, Carina saw very little of Philip at work and a couple of times at church or passing in the apartment lobby. He called or texted every day, and the days slipped by quickly. "I miss seeing you," he said one night after days of passing glimpses across campus or in the museum.

"Me, too," she said. "I think the kids' program is finally settling into a rhythm so my days should go back to some semblance of normalcy."

"I hope so," he said. "Maybe we can squeeze in lunch tomorrow?" They made plans to try.

Her schedule cleared early and she headed to his office a little before eleven the next morning, hoping the early start would give them a chance to get to the café before the regular lunch crowd. As she turned into the hallway above the gallery, she heard an unfamiliar female voice coming from his office.

His text earlier that morning told her his entire morning was open, so she decided to simply stick her head in the door to let him know she was free. Timing is everything, fate seemed to say, as the slender, tall, auburn-haired beauty, patted Philip's chest laughing at whatever clever statement he'd just made. "T*u as* *raison mon amour*." Carina's visits to France as a child and teen meant she recognized the affection in the woman's words. She stepped back quickly, but not before he spotted her.

"Carina, come in," he called. "This is Vivienne. We met in grad school. She's appraising the latest collection the Mansfields acquired. Vivienne, this is Carina Whitley. She is Mr. Mansfield's Executive Assistant and is also organizing the children's art classes we're offering."

"So nice to meet you, Carina. Philip here is quite a handful, I'm sure you agree." Not waiting for Carina's reply, she offered each cheek to Philip, who returned her kisses. The European custom, so common yet different in varying regions, was familiar to Carina. Familiarity didn't make it any easier to watch. "I must go or I shall miss my plane," she said. "We will talk soon."

Philip walked her down the hall, whispering to Carina as he passed, "Be right back."

"Take your time," she said. He frowned. Returning within a minute, he saw her sitting across from his desk, back straight, arms crossed, foot swinging rhythmically. She was upset. He smiled.

"I'm starving, Carina," he said. "Are you ready to go?" When she stood, he grabbed her hand and pulled her close. Tilting her chin up he frowned. "Look at me, please ma'am," he said. When she did, he proceeded to look in her eyes, turning her face first to the right, then to the left.

"Yes. That's a relief," he said. "They're still blue."

"My eyes?" Confusion filled her words.

"Yes. For a minute there I would've sworn they

were green." He kissed her soundly. "Jealously is a good look on you, though not one I want to see often." He straightened the papers on his desk, then led her downstairs. "She's an old friend, nothing more, besides being a bit of a gossip. Perhaps next time she's in town, we can call Sebastian Arnez to see if we can set them up on a date. You wouldn't mind seeing the handsome chef again, would you?" When he saw the smile Carina couldn't hide, he laughed. "Of course, "Of course, Vivienne's husband might take offense."

Philip settled into the chair across from Carina's desk. She locked the file cabinet, turned off her computer, and straightened the papers in her in-box before finally glancing his way. A blush swept across her cheeks. "Why are you grinning at me?"

"You are my favorite person," he said as he stood and stretched. "It's been a long day and watching you brings me joy, so I don't want to apologize for grinning." He pulled her into his arms and kissed her.

"You do look tired," she said. "If you want to put off our plans, we can."

This free weekend was their first since the end of the semester meant they'd planned to tackle the storage unit. Carina knew what furniture it contained and knew some boxes were labeled, but there were several that needed unpacking before decisions were made to save their contents. Philip knew the potential for it to be an emotional task, and had insisted she let him help.

"No, I'm fine," he said, "now. I'm looking forward to the weekend and you've promised me ice cream after I help you."

"You are a child," Carina said as they headed to the

elevator. Knowing they had a couple hours of daylight left, they stopped for a quick burger meal before heading to the storage facility. Carina only wanted to inventory the furniture, check the labeled boxes, and take the few unmarked ones to the apartment to open.

"I should donate this furniture but I really love it. I've always dreamed of an extra bedroom with the antique dresser and headboard from my grandparents." Carina sighed as she ran fingers across the intricately carved pieces. "I was sad my apartment was too small for the China cabinet. I would've loved to display their wedding dishes. Those are in one of these boxes that should be labeled." With gathered resolve she told Philip she'd look for a place to donate the furniture, but wanted to keep the dishes. Several boxes of clothes and housewares were opened and tagged for donation. Philip put the two un-labeled boxes into his car.

"Let me have the key and code for the facility and I'll handle the furniture," he said. "I'll get Jay to help me. His truck is large enough." He watched her small nod and resisted telling her his plans, hoping she'd forgive him eventually.

After the promised ice cream, they settled on her sofa with the two mystery boxes.

One contained surprisingly well-preserved baby clothes with a note in her mom's handwriting. The 'Save or Donate?' made Carina laugh.

"This is so my mother," she said. "I have vague memories of Daddy laughing at her inability to get rid of my old clothes. He even had me try to put on one of the toddler outfits." As they admired the workmanship of many of the outfits, she added, "I'll see if Emmie wants any of these, or knows anyone who could use them."

Philip opened his mouth to offer an alternative, changed his mind quickly, and changed the subject. "Your dad's vinyl collection is priceless," he said. "Jay would love those, too."

"Perfect," Carina said as she let him cut the tape on the last box, the smallest of all the ones in storage. An envelope was taped to a carefully wrapped package inside. It said simply *'For my dearest Carina.'* Carina recognized her grandmother's handwriting from seeing it on the back of photos uncovered while her aunt and uncle were visiting. Philip knew her grandmother had passed away a couple years before her parents' accident. He offered to open it and she nodded, blinking away the first tears he'd seen all day.

"Shall I read it to you?" Another nod. Scanning it quickly, he pulled her closer.

> *Dearest Carina, your arrival has brought me more joy than I can ever express. I began stitching this when your mom let me know she was expecting. I've left it in the hoop I used and I hope you leave it as is to display it, for a very special reason. When I was young, I would sit by my mom while she embroidered. One time I was looking at the work from my vantage point on the floor and made a childish comment. "That's ugly, Momma." Rather than being offended, my mother pulled me onto her lap.*
>
> *"Yes, dear, this side isn't very pretty," she said as she let me run my*

fingers over the barely recognizable pattern on the underside of the fabric. "From down on the floor it looks quite a mess, but this side shows that it's going to turn out very lovely. This is like life, my dear."

Philips voice shook and Carina handed him the box of tissues she had handy. He offered a watery smile of thanks, then read the rest of her grandmother's letter.

"There will be times in your life when it's confusing and painful...sort of like the poking of the needle as I sew, and it doesn't look like it's going to anything good. But this side, dearest, looks better and will be beautiful." Your great-grandmother's next words were a treasure. *"In our lives we need to remember that it's our Heavenly Father in charge of everything and that He loves us very, very, very much. The picture He's making will always turn out beautiful, even if it doesn't seem that way when we look at it from our viewpoint. Always trust that He has the best view and His love will make all thing, even the ugly ones, better."*

Philip folded the letter carefully as Carina unwrapped the embroidery hoop. The piece featured a garden with wildflowers and the Bible verse, "Consider how the wildflowers grow..."

The pair sat in silence for several minutes, Philip cradling Carina, until she started to giggle.

"Did you hear that?" Carina lifted her head.

"Yes, I did," Philip said. "I'm surprised the neighbors didn't call. Are you hungry? You didn't eat anything but some fries and then gave me half of your ice cream. I'll make you a sandwich." He settled her away from him, then hesitated. "If you're okay?"

"I'm okay," she said. "Better than okay, really. A feeling of connection and hope seems to have finally settled in." She leaned in for a kiss. "Thank you, Philip."

Chapter 23
The sooner, the better

The planned Fourth of July reunion gave him a target date. Well before students returned to campus, and with enough time for the summer programs to be running successfully, it was ideal. Emilia, Tess, and their husbands plotted along with him, covering for his secret meetings with a realtor and picking up a large package from a downtown gallery, and signing for the special delivery from Carina's aunt and uncle.

Two weeks after the summer programs started, Philip told Carina he needed her input on a collection. "I need a female's viewpoint," he said.

"Sure," she said. "When?"

They made plans for the following afternoon, and decided to have dinner out afterwards. "We've both been so busy that our only dates have been board games, babysitting at Jay and Emmie's or museum events," Philip said. "I know your aunt and uncle are coming back from overseas this week to sign the contract on their house. I'm guessing they'll come visit for a few days, even if the family reunion's only a couple of weeks away?" When she nodded, he added, "Since you haven't seen them since Mother's Day, I want you to have as much time with them as possible. So, if I can steal a few minutes this afternoon I'd appreciate it."

When they drove into the neighborhood, Carina recognized it. "Isn't this the area where we looked at a house for you-know-who?" she said.

"Yup," Philip said as he turned into the driveway. "This was the house. The new owner has some artwork I want you to look at. He had some questions about pieces he's thinking about for various rooms. They left a key at the office for me." He smiled.

"I still love this house," Carina said. "I dream about it sometimes. Too bad it's no longer available, although it's way out of my price range."

Philip led her inside and waited while she wandered the now empty space. "Where's the artwork you want me to see? It looks like they haven't moved anything in down here yet. I loved the view from upstairs. Should I look there first?"

"Sure," Philip said. "I'm going to check a couple pieces for the guy, too." While she wandered through the upstairs rooms, hopefully distracted by the artwork Tess had borrowed to help the ruse, Philip retrieved a painting from the hall closet and placed it on the mantel. When she circled back to the stairway, he was at the bottom, watching her. She gasped as she saw the painting.

"That's the painting I saw at the gallery we visited last week." A Saturday trip to downtown had ended at a local art gallery where Carina fell in love with a large watercolor painting that reminded her of their beach walk. "You bought it?" She started down the stairs. "And it's reframed. It looks so nice!"

"Yes, I did," Philip said as waited for her to reach him. "The painting is yours, and I had it reframed based on your expertise. I'm glad you approve. The gaudy gold filigree frame at the gallery didn't express the simplicity and beauty of the scene. Don't I sound professional?"

"Very," she said as she reached the bottom step and slipped her arms around his neck. "Do I get to take it with me today?"

"Nope," Philip said and watched her try to hide a pout. "It stays with the house. My house...or more accurately, hopefully, I dare say nervously....our house." He let her process for a moment. "I bought the house. The painting and the house are yours...well, technically it will be yours as soon as I add your name to the title. Do you know how much paperwork it takes to change a real estate title? I opted to rent to own until everything's settled. I was hoping that could happen by the Fourth of July while your family's here." He watched her confusion turn to suspicion. "That'd be too soon for a ceremony, right, but maybe not too soon for an engagement party?"

He paused as understanding dawned in her eyes. He lifted her hand to his lips, then retrieved the small box from his suit pocket. "I love you Carina. Like the painting, you frame my life now. You changed my perspective on forgiveness, love, life. I'm not complete without you, I want to be by your side, to walk through life with you. Please, please will you save me from myself and marry me?"

The ring inside brought tears to her eyes. "It's my mom's ring. How? When? Where did you find it?"

"Your aunt and uncle located it," he said, knowing they'd reveal the whole story to her later. He waited while she processed. "You haven't answered my question. Will you marry me?"

"If I must," she said, tempering her teasing with a kiss. "I love you Philip. You have had my heart from the moment I saw you. I'm sorry it took me so long to believe it, and even longer to admit it."

"No apologies needed." He sealed his reply with a kiss.

They spent the rest of the afternoon exploring their new home before enjoying a romantic dinner across town. "So are we going to tell them tonight?" Carina asked. "Did they know what was happening today?"

Philip revealed the behind-the-scenes work done by the Lazlos and Staffords. "It was impressive how we kept it secret from Sasha and also how many times we almost got caught," he said. "You have an uncanny ability to show up in places when you're not expected. I think it's another one of your superpowers."

As dessert arrived, Philip's phone began to buzz. "They're demanding an answer. Shall we tease them? I can respond with a crying face."

"Hand me your phone, sir," Carina said. "Don't be mean." She texted a response. *She said 'Yes, If I must.'"*

Laughing, cheering, thumbs up, and heart responses flooded in. Philip's mom ventured the question on everyone's mind. *Did you set a date? We'll all be here for the Fourth. Hint, hint.*

The family Independence Day celebration turned into "Losing your independence celebration," according to Jay. Emilia threw a fully loaded hotdog at him. He ducked. It landed safely in front of Carina's uncle. Apologies and laughter all around.

Despite the lobbying by the family, and their own wishes, Philip and Carina agreed that a proper wedding required more than a few days' planning. They snuck away from the family crowd before the community fireworks display began.

"I vaguely recall," Philip said, stretching the truth since he remembered the conversation clearly, "a time when you said your favorite holiday was Christmas."

"Yes, it is," Carina said. "Are you thinking what I'm thinking?"

"White and blue Christmas Wonderland, or holiday greenery and red poinsettias?" Philip kissed her gently. "You're the art expert, so which do you prefer?"

"Antique Christmas cards as wedding invitations and framed as table centerpieces," she said, then added, "Not that I've thought about it or anything."

"That's your story and you're sticking to it, I see. I'll bet there's a checklist somewhere in your apartment, desk, purse, or all three, correct? You're adorable." A pause to kiss her again stretched longer than intended. Noise from the family's picnic area brought them back to the task.

"It would be nice to have a date to give the family while they're here this weekend," Carina said. "Details like decorations can be decided later."

"I may or may not have checked the museum calendar," Philip said. "Right after the end of the fall semester, there's a weekend open."

"Of course you did," Carina said. "It's going to be a busy semester with all the new programs starting." Pulling back, she bit her lip and turned away. "Weddings involve a lot of planning. I think we should wait until the following December." She peeked at his expression.

He sputtered. "*Next* December? Are you joking? I'm not sure I'll survive." Seeing her grinning now, he tugged her back into his arms. "Not funny, Carina. Please tell me you're not serious."

"I'm not serious. The sooner the better, I think," she said, "but our families would be hurt if we eloped. I'd love a December wedding. The details will work themselves out. Big or small, fancy or not, as long as you're the one at the end of the aisle."

"That's one detail I can handle."

Epilogue

The mid-December wedding welcomed close family and friends to the small chapel near campus. Soft candlelight, vintage cards tucked into pink poinsettias and ivory-colored roses gave the ceremony a fairy tale feel. The reception, held at the museum, mirrored the theme with reprints of masterpieces reframed in antique frames.

Carina discovered a local shop, owned by the same family for generations, that had so many frames available, she spent days deciding. Philip finally convinced her to buy enough to give one to each guest. They worked together choosing which picture to give to everyone. They included a note for each, with the sentiment that conveyed their journey and romance, and how it reflected the love of their Heavenly Father.

By faith we understand that the worlds were framed by the Word of God, so that the things which are seen were not made of things which are visible. (Hebrews 11:3)
God framed the worlds, and continues to perfectly prepare, restore, and equip us…
Thank you for celebrating with us today!
Carina & Philip Corelli

A note from the Author

Reframing Love was tough to write, but I hope it was a blessing to you. I have several friends who have suffered situations like—and some much, much worse—than Carina's childhood. They have drawn hope and healing from the overwhelming love of their Heavenly Father. Even unbelievable grief and trauma can be laid at His throne and His promises can bring comfort.

Loving family and friends are vital, and often unexpected relationships bring unexpected hope, healing, and sometimes...romance.

Thank you for sharing this journey with me. I pray that no matter whatever you're facing, or have faced, you can find comfort, healing, hope, and eventually joy that comes from the love of God.

...To give them beauty for ashes, the oil of joy for mourning, the garment of praise for the spirit of heaviness... Isaiah 61:3